RUAPEHU*
A NOVEL OF NEW ZEALAND

Jesse Reiss

**Maori: exploding pit*

for

Gaynor

AUTHOR'S NOTE

The prologue is a true story,
based on accounts from the living.

The rest is purely fiction,
based on real places
and inspired by real people.

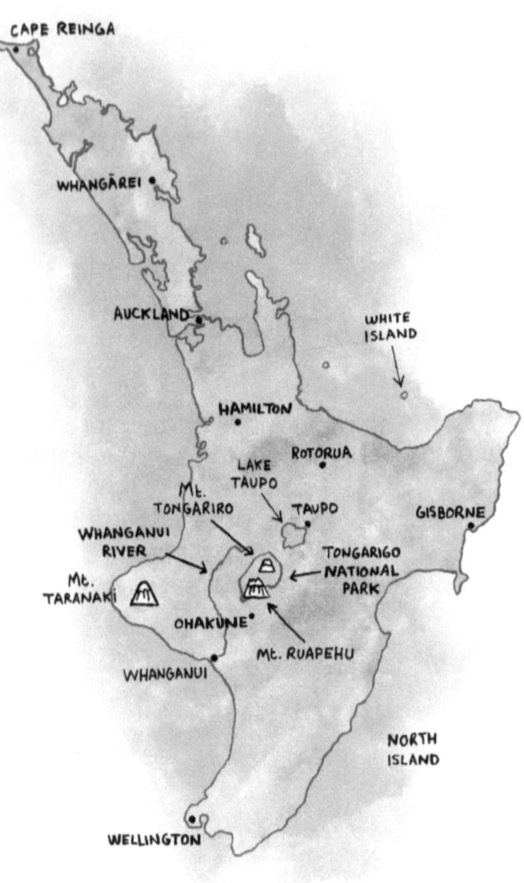

NEW ZEALAND'S NORTH ISLAND

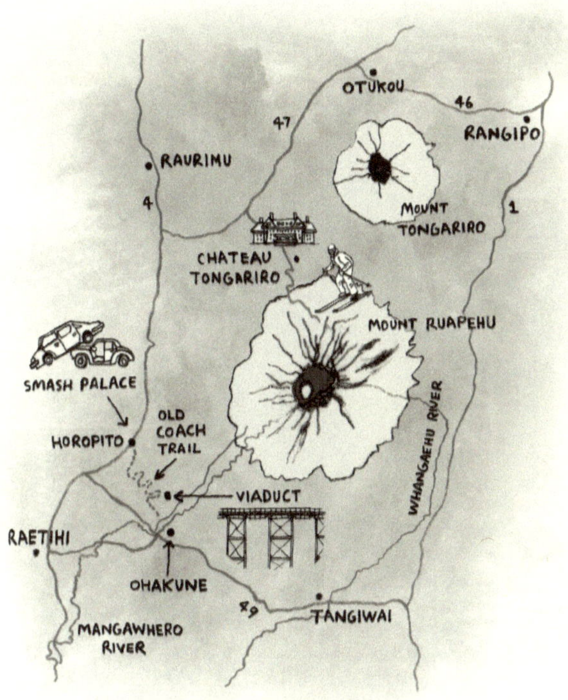

RUAPEHU MOUNTAIN VICINITY

RUAPEHU

A NOVEL OF NEW ZEALAND

TABLE OF CONTENTS

Ka Mate Haka

Kikiki! Kakaka!
Kauana kei waniwania taku tara
kei tarawahia, kei te rua i te kerokero!
He pounga rahui te uira
ka rarapa ketekete kau ana
To peru kairiri mau au e koro e!
Hi! Ha! - Ka wehi au ka matakana,
ko wai te tangata kia rere ure tirohanga
ngā rua rerarera
ngā rua kuri kakanui i raro! Aha ha!
Ka mate, ka mate! ka ora! ka ora!
Ka mate! ka mate! ka ora! ka ora!
Tēnei te tangata pūhuruhuru
Nāna nei i tiki mai whakawhiti te rā
Ā, upane! ka upane!
Ā, upane, ka upane, whiti te ra!

(English translation)
Let your valor rise! Let your valor rage!
We'll ward off these haunting hands
while protecting our wives and children!
For thee, I defy
the lightning bolts of hell
while my enemies stand there in confusion!
O God – to think I would tremble
to a pack of wolves seeing fear, or running away,
because they would surely fall in the pit of shame
as food for the hounds who chow down in delight!
Oh, what in the name…?
'Tis death! 'tis death! (or: I may die)
'Tis life! 'tis life! (or: I may live)
'Tis death! 'tis death! 'Tis life! 'tis life!
This is the hairy man
Who summons the sun and makes it shine
A step upward, another step upward!
A step upward, another... the Sun shines!

PROLOGUE

Christmas Eve, 1953

The citizens of New Zealand were overjoyed at the arrival of England's new young monarch and her handsome husband. Queen Elizabeth would be spending Christmas in the most distant part of the Commonwealth as part of her tour of the Southern Hemisphere. The country was looking up, war had been over for almost a decade and the boom of childbirths and a growing economy showed a promising future. A nation with just under two million people, but land and natural wealth rivaling the British Isles, was eager to show its sovereign how gracious and favorable it could be. The newspapers carried every detail of her day, the greeting of dignitaries, interactions with children and parades held in her honor. The foods she ate, the things she smiled at and the responses she gave were all the subject of much gossip and speculation. Men fawned to praise and impress her and women sought to emulate and please her. For a chance to see one of the largest celebrities the planet had to offer without having to leave their remote island, the people of New Zealand planned trips from distant towns and rural communities to coincide with the Queen's travels.

As it was Christmas Eve, the evening Express Train 626 from Wellington to Auckland was filled to its capacity with over two hundred and eighty excited passengers. They were heading to the northern city for their chance to see the new Queen or just to be with their loved ones on the Christmas holiday.

Driving the train was Charlie Parker, a man with over three decades of experience guiding locomotives across the country's vast rail network. An extra caboose had been added and an additional train scheduled to go an hour later to meet the demand of travelers heading to Auckland. Now after 10pm and a couple hours into the journey, voices had begun to quiet, children slept on their parent's laps, men played cards and some dozed or read newspapers. The train chugged through the dark night, passing through farmland and small towns, heading into the Tongariro National Park, home to three distinct volcanos. The first one the train would pass, Ruapehu, was the largest in size, with a profitable ski season and popular tourist attraction. Its few major eruptions in the previous century had caused only minor interruptions to human life on the mountain and did little to deter the commercialization of its landscape.

On his own journey north and just ahead of the train, Cyril Ellis, a young postal worker, drove his car through the calm black of night. The two-lane road was a mostly direct route skirting the foothills of Ruapehu. He would have rather done the familiar drive during the day to take in the beautiful scenery of the volcanic mountains in the Tongariro Park. But it was Christmas Eve, and he wanted to arrive in Rotorua later that night, to then be driving into Auckland on Christmas Day.

As he passed signs offering him directions to Ohakune, the ski town beneath the mountain, he was reminded of last year's vacation he took atop Ruapehu, skiing on its slopes and bathing in the crater lake atop the volcano, some eight thousand feet up. The large crater lake had risen in recent years from rain and snow melt and was becoming popular with daring locals who would bath in the warm acidic water and then cool down on the snowy slopes beside the water's edge.

As he approached the Tangiwai bridge over the Wangaehu river he heard a low roar that wasn't coming from his car. He cranked down the window and began to slow the vehicle. The sound was coming from outside, like a waterfall. The car's headlights brought him an unfamiliar sight. Where he expected to see the road bridge covering a gully for runoff from mountain snowmelt, the sight was now replaced by a rolling river that had risen up over the bridge and washed over the banks. He approached slowly and braked before the rushing water, seeing the road before him had become entirely swamped. He stepped out of his car, leaving the high beams on to take in the sight, marveling at what he was seeing. He had crossed this bridge many times and was familiar with the sight of a calm stream of water several meters beneath. Now it was a raging torrent, but of unusual consistency given he could see rocks, silt, and debris being pulled along with it. He knew immediately this was coming from Mount Ruapehu, which might mean it is erupting right now or something else was going on with the mountain. He looked up to where the mountain would be, but saw only darkness. He surmised that what was the crater lake atop Ruapehu had broken away, releasing thousands of tons of sulphuric water in a raging lahar that was now rushing down the mountain.

He returned to his car and brought out his torch from the glove compartment, shining it across the water, seeing trees and boulders swirling amongst the thick silt-filled water that roared past at a rapid pace as gravity tore it along its path.

He shone the torch up to the rail bridge a hundred meters further up the slope from the road bridge he had arrived at. His jaw went slack, and his stomach twisted. Two of the piers supporting the railway had given way from the impact of the lahar and were twisted, the metal girders and rail lines above them pulled out from their usual tracks like loose teeth from a jaw. He watched as the surging water made the disconnected pillars sway ever so softly, like a tree branch in a breeze.

He realized this natural disaster had only just happened, and he was the first to arrive—a lone witness to this amazing force of nature. He quickly decided to turn around and go to the nearest town he had passed several kilometers back and get warnings out and alert authorities to do something about the damage this would be causing here and further downstream. Shaking from adrenaline, he got back into his car and looked into the rearview mirror to reverse from the water's edge. As he did so he caught a faint glow of a distant moving light. He turned his head and looked through the rear window to try to figure out what it was. It appeared again, stronger and disappeared. He stepped out of the car and strained to see it again.

Yes, a locomotive was coming down the rail toward the broken bridge. Its headlight was now clearly visible, maybe a kilometer away. It must be the evening train from Wellington, likely filled with passengers. The recognition of what could happen when it reached the bridge hit him and he felt the inside of his body spasm.

Before he knew what he was doing, he had abandoned his car and was scrambling up the embankment towards the rail line and the broken bridge. Torch in hand, he reached the short fence that ran parallel to the tracks. Shoving his torch in his belt, he scrambled atop the fence and dropped to the other side. He was panting already as he ran up the gravel embankment and onto the tracks. He began to run towards the oncoming train, his flashlight held out before him, hoping it could be seen as a warning sign. As he ran he screamed repeatedly as loud as he could for the train to stop, knowing it was likely pointless. Out of the dark, the light and sound of the train came toward him as a steadily growing specter.

At the control stand of the driver's cab of Express 626, Charlie Parker monitored the steadily moving locomotive, listening to the familiar rhythmic thrum of the engines and clatter of the wheels as they glided over the rails. The train's headlight pulled distant trees, brushes and fencing into view as they approached the Tangiwai bridge, a familiar location on the route that took them beside Ruapehu mountain. As he strained into the dark ahead for the first sign of the bridge, he was puzzled by a shimmering on the ground on the right side of the track far ahead. Charlie squinted his eyes and blinked a couple times quickly, but the image didn't change. It could only be the reflection of water he thought, as if a pond had appeared up ahead beside the train tracks where he knew no natural water reservoir should be. He had driven this route numerous times in the dark and something told him what he was seeing meant something was wrong, He released the throttle, and the train began to lose momentum. He strained his eyes further, hoping for something to make sense.

Then he saw a light on the tracks ahead, a pin prick at first, like a firefly dancing across his vision. As the train approached, he saw it was a torch, and it was being held by a man running towards him, one of his arms waving frantically. The man was yelling something which Charlie could not hear over the locomotive engine. A hundred meters behind the man was the Tangiwai bridge. Charlie didn't hesitate. He slammed on the brakes and braced himself for the jolt as the train began to suddenly decrease in speed. He yelled for his fellow engineer to assist in stopping the train. He took in the stranger's face as they shot past him seconds later. He saw a mix of fright and despair as the man stepped to the side of the tracks, his shoulders and arms slumping.

Cyril had run as fast as he could toward the oncoming train, jumping between each rail tie, screaming at the top of his lungs and aiming his torch wildly. He jumped aside at the last moment and watched as the locomotive blasted past him, its wheels sliding on the rails, sparks flying up from the sand pouring onto the rails as the engineer attempted to gain friction to stop the hundred tons of steel barreling toward the bridge.

After the engine and oil tank passed, Cyril watched as carriages filled with people rumbled by. He looked up and could see a man in spectacles with a newspaper spread open. A girl with her eyes closed, face pressed against the glass, asleep. A women was chatting with another man, her eyes lost in his. Scores of passengers shot past, oblivious to the peril just ahead. He began to run back alongside the braking train, hoping for a miracle.

As the decelerating train approached the bridge Charlie saw through his windscreen the reason for the stranger's alarm. The churning water was near the height of the rail bridge and he could see the bridge now sagged to the left. He braced his arms against the front of the locomotive in a futile effort as it drove out onto the ailing overpass. He felt the vehicle lurch and suddenly they were in open space, off the tracks, moving through the air, the far bank of the river rushing toward him.

Cyril watched in horror as the tracks beneath the locomotive buckled and it launched out into open space and a second later collided with the far bank with a thunderous rending of metal and wood. Carriages followed like dominos, de-buckling with loud snaps of metal. They twisting left and right as they descended into the river, flung like logs over a waterfall. He watched as four carriages snapped off from each other, one by one and descended into the dark. Each one seemed to fall from the tracks slower than the first as the train came eventually to a halt.

A fifth carriage came to rest on the edge of the broken bridge, its front dangling in open space. As Cyril ran alongside the remaining carriages, passengers in the windows beside him were putting down their periodicals, awaking from their naps, stretching their arms and peering out into the dark, wondering why the train had come to a stop. One of them noticed Cyril running alongside the carriage and knocked on the glass, smiling down at him.

He reached the front carriage, his heart pounding and breathing labored. It extended out onto the bridge, dropping at a steep angle, but was locked in place by the remaining four carriages behind it, still on the tracks. From the river below he heard the shrieks of the crash victims. Hysterical screams and pleas for help came from the fallen carriages that he could barely make out in the dark as they bobbed and floated in the rushing currents. Several were smashed open, the occupants having been thrown from the vehicles into the thick cold silt that surged and swirled as gravity took it downstream.

He reached for the passenger door and pulled it open, the sound of its panicked occupants mixing with the screams of the ones below. He stepped inside, the door closing behind him. He climbed the steps into the carriage, surveying the scene. There were about two dozen people inside, all looking frightened and shocked as they had no understanding of why the train had stopped, and they were suddenly thrown forward at a steep angle. Voices were talking all at once, children were crying and men attempted to protect their wives and children from luggage that was falling from overhead compartments.

Cyril tried to catch his breath to speak, to tell them what happened and the danger they were in. But before he could get a word out there was a loud crack and the carriage lurched forward, the front end suddenly descending down, into the dark water.

Luggage poured down on the passengers as the carriage plunged several meters into the raging current and then righted itself, bobbing like a cork. Shocked and screaming passengers were tossed around in their seats, several sliding down the aisle, banging into each other. Within seconds murky water began to seep in through the bottom of the floor and window frames.

Cyril could feel the carriage swaying as it was taken along with the downstream current. He looked back and saw the steep steps he had come up were now filled with water that was rising fast.

"We're in a lahar! Break open these windows!" he commanded to a man standing near him that looked to still have some wits about him. The man, John Holman, shoved a passenger aside and got up onto the seat, bracing his arms on a hand railing as he launched the heel of his shoe against the window. The window cracked and mullion snapped. He reared back and hit it again. This time, glass and bits of wood flew out. Cyril was doing the same with another window, knocking out the pane and its frame with the heel of his shoe.

In a minute they had openings big enough for people to pass through. A couple of the men went out first and climbed onto the carriage's roof. They then began to help Cyril and John pull the passengers through the openings and assist them climbing to the roof. Some were in such a state of shock they struggled to stay upright, and a few were in hysterics, shaking and stammering, and had to be carried and lifted to the roof. Cyril found it necessary to hit one women across the face to get her to stop flailing and move. The carriage was flooded to the windows by the time it was emptied of people and the last wet and bedraggled passenger was resting atop the floating coach.

Around them they heard the desperate screams of passengers trapped in sinking carriages, their voices one by one slowly going quiet. They could hear splashing and writhing as passengers that had been thrown from the carriages attempted to swim to shore in the thick mud-filled water or got caught up in foliage along the banks and fought their way to find a firm hold. As minutes passed, the sounds of the desperate victims around them began to dim as the trapped lost the fight for their lives or the few survivors found a way to safety.

As the lahar lost its force and the level of the water began to drop, the current slowed. The carriage became wedged against the bank of the gully far from where it had entered and the water began to drain out of it. With the help of Cyril and other able passengers, the carriage occupants were able to disembark to safety on the far side of the river.

Within an hour the water was back down to a small stream, leaving a mud-soaked wreckage with carnage and mayhem stretching for hundreds of kilometers downstream.

Rescue workers and volunteers began to arrive from neighboring towns, bringing flood lights, ropes, and spades and the work began to find bodies and survivors and look for answers to questions about how the disaster had happened.

In all a hundred and fifty one souls were lost that Christmas Eve and another one hundred and thirty four were saved by the actions of Charlie and Cyril. Twenty bodies were never recovered, thought to have been carried down the river hundreds of kilometers and buried at sea.

The crust of New Zealand's North Island is among the thinnest in the world, while its many volcanos are a reminder of the sphere of lava all life as we know it sits atop—a sphere that comprises ninety-nine percent of the Earth's mass.

Given the rage and fury of which the land's geological history shows she is capable, the Tangiwai railroad disaster was but a single tear shed from the mighty Ruapehu

CHAPTER ONE

Present day

Ken Ryan kept a steady pace as he hiked the Old Coach Road trail, one of many well-planned paths in the Ruapehu mountain foothills. He was accompanied by Sabre, the family Weimaraner, a loyal and highly intelligent animal. He walked briskly up the wide path, enjoying the exercise of the moderate incline as the dog let its nose guide a zig-zag path on and off the trail. Edged by thick vegetation of native bush, the trail was well cared for with various signposts indicating directions and time estimates to popular lookouts and bridges that criss crossed the region.

He'd made trips to this land before, flying across the Pacific from his home in San Diego, and had seen the mountain under varying conditions. It stood by itself, rising majestically from flat plains in one of the oldest national parks in the world. As always, he felt the presence of the snow-capped volcanic mountain above, though on this day it was concealed by clouds.

The spring October air, far from dense city life and endless digital distractions, had been cathartic, and Ken felt relaxed and buoyant. He had come to this land of peace and green just a week earlier to be with his mother's family and help heal wounds of a decade-long marriage that had dissolved. So far the trip had been working. He'd been able to step away from his busy life of teaching, covering bills, and keeping up with social contacts.

He thought about the times he and his ex-wife made trips to New Zealand together, including with members of his close family. The last one was two years earlier with his sister to spread their mother's ashes on this very mountain. These trips contained few bad memories. The negative emotions were back when the infidelity had become known, and he had to continue to go about his life routines, erecting pretenses that his pride was still intact. The memories containing incidents through the years of late-night quarrels where no logic he proffered would penetrate, leaving him feeling he was debating a hall of mirrors. The melancholy had gotten to the point where his aunt demanded he take a few weeks off and come visit at her home near Ruapehu. He shook his head of the memories and tried to remind himself there were just as many fond memories over the years too, and he was by no means free of guilt. He was now trying to extract himself from that mess and start a rebuild of his life.

After an hour on the trail his view opened up to an abandoned large iron viaduct built to support locomotives chugging across the span of a steep valley. He read the signpost that told him the viaduct was built at the turn of the nineteenth century and replaced by a new more modern concrete one a few decades ago on a more direct line, further away. The iron structure was the width of a single-lane country road, built as one of the connecting rail lines that ran from the industrial cities at the top of New Zealand's North Island down to Wellington, the capital at the bottom.

Ken tried to imagine what it was like a hundred years before when passengers disembarked in the middle of the wilderness and were taken by stagecoach down the trail he had just walked to their next train connection. In his climb he had passed less than a dozen fellow hikers, possibly because rain was predicted later in the day or more likely this was just one of many trails around the mountain and surrounding Tongariro National Park.

He walked up to where the train tracks would have been only to see thick wooden planks nailed to the earth, covering what was once operational rails, like stitches on a wound. He looked to his left, following their path, disappearing into the darkness of a large tunnel dug into the side of the mountain. The planks went across the viaduct, which spanned a couple hundred meters and on the far side in the distance, disappeared around the side of the mountain. The viaduct spanned the width of the chasm with a network of iron trusses and girders welded together in criss-cross patterns. As the viaduct curved across the steep valley, it was a drop of more than sixty meters down to trees and a mountain stream.

Sabre had moved ahead and began to trot along the planks, stopping as he reached the start of the viaduct with its small handrails that look down into open space. Sabre looked back for confirmation, and Ken waved his arm, letting the dog know he could move ahead. The Weimaraner was a cunning animal, well trained and attentive. He belonged to Ken's aunt, Ruth Sybil. In the few days Ken had been back with them, Sabre knew he was part of the family and obeyed him like a master.

As Ken began to step from plank to plank, Sabre froze ahead of him. Ken noticed the dog's change and looked to where it was staring. A body was lying face down on the edge of the viaduct, unmoving. He tried to make sense of what he was seeing as his heart sped up. Whoever it was appeared to be lying with their head and arms slung over the edge, like they'd been tossed from a moving train, though no train or vehicle had crossed in years. He moved forward, preparing his mind for what might be a grisly scene. He could see the person was wearing ordinary sneakers, frayed jeans and a dark top.

As he got closer an ankle moved, and the shoulders pinched. The person was alive. They appeared to be bending far over the edge, and Ken could now see a strap around the neck. From the shape of the hips, Ken could see it was a girl.

Sabre had silently trotted up to the prostrated individual and began to sniff her leg. A small shriek came out as her body suddenly came to life. The strap around the neck jerked taut as she lost hold of what it was attached to and lunged forward to grab it again. Ken saw the body slide forward, the waist almost over the edge. He jumped the last several feet and grabbed an ankle. That caused an even more horrifying scream. Sabre began to bark, adding to the panic.

"I've got you!" Ken yelled, trying to sound reassuring. She began to wriggle and squirm to get back from the edge. He pulled on the ankle to help, letting go once the shoulder blades cleared the side.

An arm came up, and a large Nikon camera swung back and was placed on the edge. Then the person spun around, using the handrail above her head to slide the rest of the way to safety, her shirt pulling up to expose a firm stomach and bottom of a red bra.

A pretty woman faced him, red-faced and wide-eyed with fear and fluster. She pulled her shirt down and sat up. She wore a San Francisco Giants baseball cap concealing most of her blonde hair. She stared at him for a brief second and must have seen by his worried look that he was not a threat.

"You scared the hell out of me!" she exclaimed, shaking her head.

"Sorry," he responded with a weak apology. "I couldn't tell if you were injured, contemplating suicide or what. I didn't realize you were just taking photographs."

She appeared to recover quickly from her fright. Her shoulders relaxed, and she chuckled. "I guess it must have looked strange," she said, appearing to forgive him. She got to her feet and put out her hand. He shook it lightly. Her eyes were blue and showed confidence. She was just over five feet with a petite figure. She had a youthful face and a smile that showed a set of perfect teeth. "I'm Maya, freelancer for National Geographic."

Ken nodded, raising his eyebrows to show he was impressed. "Ken Ryan. Sorry, nothing like National Geographic. Just a school teacher out for a morning constitutional." He shrugged, trying to appear modest.

"You American?" she asked in a definite American accent of her own and with a curious shake of her head as she brushed herself off. He found himself noticing her figure and the curves under her shirt as she wiped the small bits of debris from her pants.

"Yeah, from San Diego. Here visiting my aunt for a few weeks. This is her dog, Sabre. You're also American?"

"Yeah, Monterey myself. On assignment. I went off script a bit when I saw the light patterns the bridge trusses make as it descends into the valley. Here, take a look." She picked her camera up off the tracks and turned around so he could see the screen. The first he saw was an out-of-focus blurry block of iron with an edge of green. "That was when you jumped me," she chided.

The next photos surprised him. They showed an intricate pattern of metal trusses with light rays and shadows seeming to descend into infinity. She flipped through them quickly, moving her head from side to side and scrunching her nose frequently, making her own mental evaluations as she analyzed them. A citrus scent came to Ken, and he was tempted to lean in closer. He caught himself and pulled back.

"Those are pretty cool. So National Geographic pays you to do this?" he asked, pointing to the last image.

"Nah, these are just for me. My partner and I are on an assignment connected to a future series on the Ring of Fire and people living with volcanos. After the White Island eruption, the interest in the subject spiked, and so we're doing a series on the volcanic activity through the country. Ruapehu here is one of the most active volcanos, so I'm getting to know the terrain while my partner—who's the real scientist—flies above in a two-seater getting aerial views." She looked up at the cloudy sky, "which probably isn't working out too well for her with that cloud covering."

Ken nodded, looking up, "Yeah, sometimes the weather doesn't cooperate, and you don't see the mountain for days."

"They're likely on the other side of the mountain right now or above the clouds looking down on its crown," Maya added. Her face blanched, and she looked down at the planks beneath their feet. "Is that a train coming? I thought this was abandoned?"

CHAPTER TWO

"It is abandoned," Ken replied, looking around. "The tracks are covered." And then he felt it—a low vibration that could precede an on-coming locomotive. He spun left and right and saw no indication of something coming.

The vibrations suddenly picked up, the entire structure pulsating as the grating sound of metal on metal assaulted their ear drums, like hail on a tin roof. His feet suddenly lost their balance, and he went to his knees on the planks, reaching out for Sabre and grabbing his collar, as the dog braced its legs and whined. Maya went down on her rear, cradling her camera as her body lightly shook and vibrated, fear in her eyes.

"An earthquake!" he yelled to be heard. The terror of the viaduct giving way and plunging them to their deaths came to him, and he made an attempt to get to his feet and move.

It was impossible. He had no chance of standing without the possibility of being thrown from the edge. Sabre whimpered loudly as Ken put his arm tight around him, fearing the dog would be thrown from the side if it bolted in panic.

"Just stay down and hold on!" Maya yelled, seeing the panic in Ken's eyes. She had a grip on one of the planks and looked determined. Ken had been in buildings during earthquakes in California and felt the fright and power of Mother Nature as solid concrete swayed and immovable objects bounced like they had springs. But on such an old and insecure structure, he had nothing with which to judge its safety.

They lay there, holding tight to the viaduct, listening to it groan, clank, and creak as birds took flight and the deep rumbling filled their ears. Sabre attempted a few times to get up and run, sliding Ken along the ground, the panic in him rising higher. He feared sliding off the side or the track falling away with them attached, like ants on a dead branch.

Half a minute passed before the shaking let up, and stability slowly returned. The viaduct had held with no immediate visible damage. Dust had risen up around them, making them cough.

Gingerly, Ken got to his knees and looked over at Maya. She was doing the same.

"You okay?" he asked.

"Yeah, I'm alright. Little shaken up, but okay. There's no getting familiar with earthquakes. I hate them."

"Let's get off this thing before any aftershock comes," Ken said.

She nodded in agreement, and they stood up together.

Holding tight to Sabre's collar, they went back the way they came, carefully watching each plank to be sure they weren't going to trip or plunge to their death on one that may have come loose. The viaduct was surprisingly intact, like nothing had happened. Each step felt closer to safety until they reached solid ground, and relief swept through them. Ken moved to the grass and slumped to the ground to steady himself and catch his breath. His head was dizzy, and his body shook from the fright.

"What an experience! I'm not sure if I was more afraid of being jumped by you or being tossed off the bridge!" She laughed, which made Ken do the same. It was a relief.

They sat on the grass, Sabre nuzzling into Maya, sniffing her, and putting his wet nose on her face. She scratched him behind the ears and made cute faces, which got his tail wagging. She had recovered from the shock so quickly it took Ken by surprise. She was very pretty he noticed, and he felt awkward in wanting to talk to her, but not sure what to say.

She caught him looking at her with curiosity on his face. She raised an eyebrow, and he was suddenly off guard, so said something that he realized sounded stupid as it came out. "You know this is the same bridge the first bungee jumper in New Zealand leapt from?"

"It's cursed," she responded with a wink, giving Sabre a final pat.

"Earthquakes are a natural occurrence in this country, as you probably know," he added. "But I've never been here before when one hits." He was trying to sound calm, though he could still hear tremors in his own voice.

"Yeah, this ties into our research and reporting," Maya responded. "New Zealand gets over a hundred quakes a year, all part of the plate movements that first formed these islands and that huge volcano we are sitting under. Couldn't have been a better time for me to be here. Not what you probably wanted for your morning 'constitutional.'" She put the finger quotations in the air with a warm smile, and Ken wasn't sure whether to be embarrassed for using a big word or amused by the ease with which she playfully mocked him.

She then pulled out her cell phone, becoming businesslike. "I've gotta call my partner up there who no doubt will want to get reports and statements from seismologists and such. We've also got some interviews we want to do later today and in a few days head up to the mud pools at Rotorua." She put the phone to her ear, her fears forgotten, and a second later she was looking out to the horizon, talking. "Yeah! Yeah... I was on an old bridge when it just happened..."

Ken paid some attention to the conversation, fascinated by the science lingo being tossed around and the day-to-day workings of a nature journalist on assignment. He took notice she wore no wedding ring and had painted her nails a crimson color. He chastised himself for noticing and tried to distract himself by taking over the petting of Sabre. After a few minutes, he was lost trying to follow the acronyms and references to an unknown world and laid back in the grass and closed his eyes, thankful to be alive.

A few minutes later he realized she must have ended the call as her voice had gone quiet. He heard the sound of a camera shutter and opened his eyes. Maya was standing beside him and had just taken his photo. She slowly lowered the camera. "That okay?" she asked.

He narrowed his eyes and paused for effect, and then nodded. "Sure," he said, sitting up. He pulled out his own phone, aiming it at her. She put her hands on her hips and pursed her lips to one side, posing. He smirked and took a couple of her. If he wasn't crazy, she was flirting with him.

"Okay, Mr.?"

"Ryan. Ken Ryan," he replied nervously.

"Right! Well, Mr. Ryan, it's been a real pleasure to meet you in such wild circumstances. My day somehow got even more exciting with this happening, so I've got to get moving since I am technically the one at work here."

They said goodbye with an awkward handshake, her going down one path and he another. Sabre and Ken watched her going, her camera across her shoulders, absorbed in her cell phone. Sabre tugged hard at the leash, wanting to follow. Ken realized he hadn't asked for a number or even her last name. He knew she was working for National Geographic, so could possibly track her down and reach out to her. He realized he was drawn to more than just her slim figure and gentle curves. He was enamored by her independence and self-control.

As he pondered this he realized the craziness with what he was thinking. He hardly knew anything about her. He was here to get away from all this and get over a divorce, not kindle something with a stranger he'd just met.

CHAPTER THREE

"**D**id you feel the little tremor?" Ruth Sybil cheerfully asked as Ken entered through the sliding glass door and back into her home. His aunt was sitting on the couch with her feet up and a cup of tea, greeting a jubilant Sabre who darted for her, his tail threatening to knock over anything not solidly fixed to the floor.

"Little?! Are you kidding? We were on that abandoned bridge on the Old Coach Road when it happened. Almost tossed me off the side. The thing shook violently. I feared I was going to die."

"Oh, my, that must have been a fright! Well, it was a 3.9 per the GeoNet tracker. Caused a little shaking around the house, nothing major. Some plates rattled, but nothing fell or broke. Must have been far worse on that viaduct." She pronounced it *veerduck*.

Ruth was a quintessential Kiwi. An amply proportioned and well-freckled lady with a confident demeanor, always talking in certainties with a sensible business mind. Her vivacious personality was half the reason Ken had taken the offer to visit her. She'd gained and lost, and regained businesses, husbands, and homes and still found ways to laugh at the world and herself. He needed to find that for himself.

"Well, the thing did seem fine afterward," he reflected. "Must be built with that sort of event in mind. I met a photographer on the bridge, and she was showing me some of her shots when the whole thing started shaking. We thought a train might be coming." He went on to describe how it felt like the top of a skyscraper during a major shake.

"Sounds like you need a cuppa," Ruth replied and offered him tea and some biscuits. They spent the afternoon in conversation and preparing some rooms for her daughter and family who were due to arrive in a couple days from Auckland for a long weekend. The home was a two-level country lodge with a wooden deck around two sides that faced the mountain. The home had a few bedrooms with large windows wrapping around the ground floor. Green lawns and gardens gave way to shrubs, wild bush, and the surrounding countryside. Ruth's was one of several homes in the hamlet of Horopito, most famous for Smash Palace, a large car graveyard you had to drive through to get to her place.

Ruth explained to Ken there were rabbits infesting the vegetables again and asked that he get up early with Sabre when they are most active and shoot as many as possible. She showed him the bedroom closet where rifles and ammo were kept and ensured he knew the intricacies of the particular weapons. Sabre was bred to hunt them she explained and described the body language he would display and commands he knew to obey.

Ken was happy to help with the task of removing the cute vermin, but didn't consider himself a hunter with the stomach to kill anything bigger.

As they were discussing this, there was the sound of a car on the gravel driveway and a double honk. "That's Brodie, my employee," Ruth said. "Can you grab the two jars of honey sitting on a bench in the back and bring them in?"

Ken went out back and found the two mason jars where she said they would be. Ruth had gathered the raw honey from her personal apiary located on the property. Various insects were clamoring on the jars, and flies buzzed around. He turned on a nearby hose, rinsed them down, and returned to the house with them wrapped in a towel.

He was met in the living room by a wide-chested Maori gentleman a head taller than he was with thick arms and hands. Ken estimated he was in his late 20s. He wore a "Quicksilver" shirt with cut-off sleeves that showed tattoos that started at his forearms and worked their way in elaborate patterns up to his neck. He wore cargo pants, and his feet were bare but dark-skinned and leathery.

"Kai ora! You must be Ken," he gregariously said with a deep New Zealand accent. "Brodie Savennu here."

"Yes," Ken said, shaking the proffered hand with a smile and then handing the jars over to him. "Pleased to meet you," though he was more intrigued and curious about the man.

Brodie nodded agreeably. "Ruth said you were visiting from the States. So cool."

"Brodie here is the tech guru of our little business," Ruth explained with a smile. "Handles all the internet stuff and can be some extra muscle when we need it."

He was visibly embarrassed by the praise, trying to hide a toothy grin with a downcast shake of the head. "Just happy to have work," he replied. "What do you do back in the big U.S. of A?" Brodie asked, trying to politely turn the topic away from him.

"I teach at a high school. Academics," Ken responded with a shrug.

"Oh yeah, didn't get enough of that myself," Brodie acknowledged with a chuckle. He raised his eyebrows, "But I could teach you the Haka while you're here," he said with an eager nod.

Ken was reminded of his first experience with the Maori Haka when he was just four years old, and on one of the trips he had made with the family to New Zealand, they had gone to a performance of the ritual. His grandparents had warned him it might be scary and offered to stay outside with him while the rest of the family went in. Ken had reasoned if they could brave it, so could he. When the performance started, he found little to fear and was more in awe at the display of raw emotion and directed force. "Oh, I don't have the tattoos for that," Ken said with a laugh.

Brodie smiled and shook his head, "It's not the tattoos Bro. It's all up here," he said, pointing to his head. "And here," he said, putting his hand on his heart. He gave Ken a serious nod of the head to convey his meaning. "When you are performing the Haka, it is a humbling and very spiritual experience. You may appear angry and terrifying on the outside, but as a being you feel out of your body and very alive."

Ken nodded in understanding. He admired the modesty of such an imposing and physical presence. He often saw similar-looking athletes in America with egos and swagger in their walk, full of unfounded confidence. But, as with most of the Maoris he met, he'd found them to be humble and gentle people, their politeness incongruous with their outward appearance, similar to what Brodie was describing.

"When the ski season ends in a few weeks," Ruth explained, "Brodie performs regularly with his tribe for tourists and locals at Chateau Tongariro. It's quite a show. And yes, those tattoos and muscle definitely help," she added with a flex of her arm.

Ruth and Ken watched from the porch as Brodie left down the steps with the jars of honey. "Call on me if you need anything, aye?" he said back to Ken. "Ruth's got my number. I've lived here my whole life and would love to show you some of the cool spots, you know? Stuff tourists don't see. That'd be fun, aye?"

"Sure," Ken said with a wave, wondering if the invitation had a catch he missed or if it was just natural for people to be this friendly here. He realized from past experience with trips to New Zealand, it was probably the latter.

As the afternoon wore on and the sun began to drift to the horizon, they got the fireplace going, attracting Sabre to doze on the hearth. Ruth began to prepare supper as Ken drifted through emails and news on his laptop.

After what seemed like an hour of silence, Sabre got up from where he was sleeping, sniffed the air, and let out a low growl. Ruth came out of the kitchen and spoke to him. "What is it, Boy"?

The dog went up to the glass door and began to bark, his tail wagging furiously. "Must be someone he knows nearby," she explained to Ken. "See that tail going. Usually neighbors walking up the path. They sometimes bribe him with a little treat. I'll let him out." She slid open the door, and he darted out, bounding down the steps, out of sight around to the front of the house.

A moment later, Ruth called from the kitchen, "Um, Ken, is this your photographer friend coming up the drive?"

CHAPTER FOUR

Ken quickly put down his laptop and went to the kitchen to look out the window. Sure enough, Maya and another older lady with short grey hair were walking up the drive. Sabre was latched to Maya, attempting to get as much affection as he could.

Ruth gave Ken a little elbow in the ribs. "You could have mentioned she was a little bombshell."

Ken didn't have time to respond as Ruth stepped out onto the porch of the house, "Hello! Can I help you?" she asked, looking down at the arriving ladies.

They stopped where they were, and the older lady spoke up to her in an American accent "Oh, hello. My name is Cynthia. Maya it appears has already met your dog," she added with a friendly chuckle. "We're nature journalists from National Geographic, doing research on the environment, and we're hoping we could briefly interview the owner of the property."

Ruth sounded curious, "That would be me, Ruth Sybil. What is this for?"

"Well, a Google Maps survey of the Ruapehu mountain and Tongariro Park shows this to be one of the closest living homes to it. We are hoping to be able to get a feel for what it is like for the residents living close to an active volcano."

"Oh, okay. Sure, come on in," Ruth replied matter of factly. "I was just fixing a feed. I hope you haven't eaten. I can throw in a few more fish. No problem." As they began walking up the stairs, she headed back into the house not looking to see if either indicated they were ready to eat. She turned back to them as they were coming up the steps. "We can talk and eat at the same time, while we watch to see if Ruapehu might toot her horn for us, aye?" She laughed and got a smile from everyone. They entered the home, and she headed back to the kitchen.

Maya gave an awkward smile at Ken as she stepped into the house and raised her hands in mock surrender. "Hello again. I had no idea you lived here, honestly. A few days ago, we located some homes in this area of the park on the internet and randomly chose to visit them."

Ken smiled and shook his head, making nothing of it. "It's a small country," he replied. "San Diego area has more people than this entire country. You can expect to run into someone more than once."

"Hi, I'm Cynthia," said the older lady, putting out her hand. Ken shook it and smiled. "Pleased to meet you. Maya and I met earlier today," he added.

"Yes, I heard it was quite the experience, the two of you holding onto each other as you were almost thrown from the viaduct."

Ken saw Maya blush out of the corner of her eye as he was about to correct Cynthia, to say he was holding onto the dog, but realized this was probably the version of events Maya intentionally mis-told her. "Yeah," Ken said, giving Maya a quizzical look, "Neither one of us might be standing here today if we didn't happen to meet each other at the same time that the quake struck." He gave Maya a conspiratorial wink, going along with her fabrication of the event, and her blush seemed to redden.

Twenty minutes later they were sitting at the patio deck with a bottle of wine and some excellent tasting homemade fish and chips. After many compliments on the food and hospitality, Cynthia explained her science background at Stanford and years spent in Yellowstone and around the Philippines. As the elder and more credentialed member of the two, Maya let her do most of the talking and explaining of their journalistic mission.

Ruth seemed delighted to be having dinner with three Americans in her home and steered the conversation this way and that, getting a feel for their views on life in the States compared to New Zealand and finding agreement on some environmental and political issues. She gave a short summary of her life running various start-ups and enterprises in Auckland, then selling out and deciding to move to the countryside and slow down, but finding herself again picking up a business renting chateaus around the mountain and various small enterprises on the side. She thought she was heading into retirement, but finds herself just as busy now as she was in the big city. She modestly brushed aside their praise at how attuned she was with world events. She told them most New Zealanders—though sometimes seeming naive—generally show a stronger interest in world events than they did in their own country. The opposite of Americans. She told them a story of visiting a home of local Maori friends to see them watching the American C-Span station as they debated the political docket amongst themselves.

The sun had begun to set, and the birds quieted. Clouds continued to obscure the mountain, drawing attention to the lower ridges and forests that made up the base, now mostly shadows. Cynthia hesitantly took out a notepad. "I'd like to ask some specific questions about what it is like living beside an active volcano."

Ruth laughed, "Oh, that sounds ominous doesn't it? Haha. Not sure if you just called me an idiot for making my home here, but I better start sounding intelligent hadn't I, aye?" She straightened her spine and adjusted her glasses. That got a chuckle from everyone.

The night was interrupted by a distant train whistle and the faint sound of a locomotive rolling over tracks. "That would be the evening train coming through to Ohakune," Ruth commented with a smile. "Runs by Horopito every night at this time."

They listened together in silence for several seconds to the faint but familiarly rhythmic sound of a distant train rolling over rails. It was interrupted by a long unpleasant screech of metal and then a crunch and then louder sounds of what could only be metal bending and sliding together in ways not intended. The sound lasted for several seconds and then the countryside around them was silent again.

CHAPTER FIVE

R uth bolted up from the table "That sounded like a train accident, right here by Smash Palace! Gosh I hope no one's hurt! Let's go!" They all moved after her as she rushed back into the house, threw on a coat, grabbed her keys, and led them out the door. Her Land Rover was parked rear-first in the drive, and she yelled for everyone to get in. They piled into the vehicle and she took off, navigating the narrow bumpy drive and onto the gravel road with the dexterity of someone who had taken the route a thousand times. She tore down the road, heading to the sound of the crash. Cynthia and Maya looked at each other with eyebrows raised, fearful at what they would find and also amazed at their luck to be firsthand witnesses to a breaking event.

Thirty seconds later they came upon Smash Palace, a graveyard of old rusted vehicles and wrecks that had collected over several acres in this part of the country for many decades. The gravel road took them around walls of stacked old cars arranged in plots beside the train track. Around the bend the train tracks came into view and they saw a train had come to a stop on the tracks, blocking them from crossing. Looking down the line from where the road intersected they could see in the dim light several well cars and containers had gone off the rails and were now lying on their sides or at odd angles from the tracks. One container had spilled open, scattering scores of boxes and thousands of oranges across the ground, like bright autumn leaves on a fall day.

At this time of night the junkyard would have been vacant. The place was run during the day by a few men who seemed to keep loose hours and were rarely seen. With only a score of neighboring houses making up the Horopito cluster of homes, the stillness and silence of the countryside had returned.

Ruth thrust her cell phone into Ken's hand telling him to dial Emergency and report the crash. Putting the vehicle in park, she grabbed a large torch from the glove box and they piled out, walking alongside the wreck, looking for signs of human life. Ruth shouted "Hello! Anyone here?!" repeatedly, waiting each time for an answer. There was only the hissing of steam and sounds of insects in the brush on either side of the tracks. They went down several well cars still sitting on the tracks and felt some relief in realizing there was little chance of live cargo on this train.

A man in light-blue overalls came around one of the well cars that had flipped on its side. He waved the hat he had in his hand at them and continued to inspect the undercarriage with his own torch. He went over to the tracks and shone his light up and down, shaking his head. They began to approach him.

"You okay Sir?" Ruth asked with much concern.

"Yeah, I'm okay. My delivery sure isn't. It's gonna take a long time to sort this one."

"No one else was aboard?"

"Nah, just me taking this delivery down to Ohakune." He waved his flashlight over the sight again and shook his head. "Anyone care for some oranges?"

It took twenty minutes for the first emergency vehicles to arrive with their lights flashing, penetrating the surrounding black of night. They were interviewed as well as a few other neighbors who came out after hearing the crash. They relayed what they heard, but with no eye witnesses, there was little else to add to what was there. It was established no one was injured, and there was nothing to be done until morning when wreckage crews would come down the line with equipment, cranes, and insurance adjustors to do their thing. As some workers came with caution tape and emergency floodlights to set up around the site, they were thanked for coming out and told they could return home.

They got back into the Land Rover for the short return, chatting about the excitement of the scene. As they approached Ruth's driveway, she stopped by a sedan parked on the side of the road. "That your rental?" she asked Cynthia.

"It is."

"You have a hotel in town?"

"Yeah."

"Darn," Ruth replied. "That wreck has trapped you. That's the only road out of this place.

Unless you've got a vehicle like mine and maybe can drive through the brush around the wreck. And even then, it's pretty rough terrain that would ruin the paint job."

They pondered this in silence.

Ruth added, "I imagine they'll have the road sorted by mid-day. In the meantime, you are welcome to stay here in a cabin I have on the property."

"That'd be really appreciated," Maya said eagerly. "I'd love to take photos of that wreck at first light."

Cynthia was more humble in accepting, offering to compensate her and further grateful when she refused the offer. Her and Maya helped Ruth and Ken clean up what was left of the dinner they had abandoned on the patio.

They walked down to a large cabin near the base of the driveway, tucked behind some trees. Ken helped them bring their bags in from their rental. The place had a fireplace and a few small rooms, some furnished with multiple bunks for family gatherings or the busy winter ski season where rooms could be rented out for weekend family getaways on the mountain slopes.

Ruth and Ken went back to the main house and returned with fresh linen and an invitation for breakfast. The two ladies were grateful and made polite attempts to be as little a burden as possible.

As Ruth was showing Cynthia how to operate the shower, Maya spoke to Ken quietly, a nervous inflection in her voice. "Look, I should apologize for making that story up about us on the bridge. I'm usually a very truthful person, and since I didn't think our paths would cross again, it was just my own stupid fantasy to make an already hard to believe story even more so. I shouldn't have made it up. I feel bad for doing that."

"Nah, that's okay," Ken said. "I thought it was cute."

"Thanks for not making me look like an ass."

The conversation abruptly ended when the two older ladies came out of the shower room, completing the tour of the cabin. Ken felt an urge to continue talking to Maya just as she had begun to show a vulnerable side and open to him. But in the presence of the two older ladies, the gracious smile had returned to her face, and he knew the evening had come to an end.

Ruth and Ken said their goodnights and headed back to the main lodge.

CHAPTER SIX

Ken rose at dawn the next morning, dressing in a warm jacket, beanie and gloves. He retrieved the gun from the closet. He loaded it in the living room, trying to clear the fog from his mind. Sabre stood wide awake, eyes fixed on him, ready for business. They quietly slipped out the sliding door and walked softly across the dew-filled grass to the gardens in the back of the house. Everything was cold and damp. He was unsure if this came from rain during the night or thick layers of dew having settled.

He noticed thick clouds still covered the sky, concealing the mountain. This was now his fourth day on this trip, and he'd yet to see the snow-capped crown. He thought he might take an afternoon to drive up to the ski slopes near the top, above the clouds. There he could do some hiking and take in the peaks. At just under three-thousand meters and with serrated teeth surrounding a large crater lake at the top, it might not be the highest volcano in the North Island, but it was the largest and most popular.

Ken scanned the couple acres of vegetable rows and fruit trees, wondering where to start. He remembered that was Sabre's job and leaned down to the dog's ear. "Where's the rabbit?" he asked in a hushed tone of excitement.

The dog took off into the garden, leaping over plants, sniffing and prowling. A few seconds later a small animal darted across several rows. It froze between two cabbage stalks, its nose twitching. Ken quickly raised the rifle and sighted it. Then another rabbit came into his peripheral vision and he switched to it, taking aim again. The rifle shot was a sharp sound, echoing into the countryside with a small kick to his shoulder. Amazingly, Sabre went over, picked up the kill in his mouth, brought it to Ken's feet, and went out searching for more. Twenty minutes later Ken had four of them at his feet.

As he was aiming for another he heard a faint shutter click and slowly looked to his left. Maya was standing there, taking his photo.

She lowered her camera and made a pistol shape and motion with her hand. "Shot you." she said with a coy smile. "But don't shoot me."

He slowly shook his head with a smile and lowered the gun. "I've done enough here," he said. "I'm not the best person to be killing little animals that have done me no harm."

"Your aunt put you up to this then?"

"Yeah. Helping de-vermin her garden. I'm going to suggest she go back to laying traps. She'd might consider that because I'm an American it must be natural for me to shoot a gun."

"I take it you're not a Republican then?" Maya asked.

"I've met you yesterday," he said with a laugh. "I don't even know your full name, and we're already having the politics talk?"

She gave him a disarming smile. "Richardson."

"Huh?"

"My last name," she said with a chuckle, "Richardson."

Ken smiled, "Thank you. Ken Ryan, as I've said before. Pleasure to meet you."

She laughed. "I'm heading down to that train wreck to shoot it in first daylight. Want to come?"

"Sure. I like watching you work," Ken replied.

She raised her eyebrows with a coy smile. "You like watching *me* or the work that I do?"

Ken blushed and gave a light shrug. "Probably both, to be honest." He returned the gun to the house, and they slowly walked the ten minutes down the road, idly talking with Sabre leading the way. Ken found himself explaining to her the family connections and lineage that brought him to this country and his own work with non-profits in San Diego to help keep youth away from vices and set them up for meaningful careers.

She was an attentive listener, asking questions that showed a deep curiosity. She shared with him her path through arts college in San Francisco and balancing being on the road and staying close to her family back in the States.

Arriving at the site, they found caution tape had been strung around the entire area with a couple perimeter officers in hardhats standing idly to the side, a small pile of orange peelings at their feet. The accident was as they left it the night before, but now in the clear morning light they could see the extent of the damage with four cabooses on their side, two of them crushed while a dozen others had derailed and were now alongside the tracks or twisted sideways.

One of the men politely approached them, bowing slightly and speaking in a polished manner. "Hello there. I'm Officer Poval. Can I be of help?"

They explained their presence at the scene the previous night and he listened, nodding earnestly.

"Oh, must have been quite a fright, I must say," he said quietly, as if apologizing on behalf of the interruption. "It appears the small tremor we had yesterday dislodged something, you see, causing one of the rails to kinda buckle up, you know." He nodded at his own knowledgable conclusion. "And that was all it took for the train coming along later to take a little tumble." He grimaced, like a father explaining a toddler's tricycle accident. With exaggerated nods, he assured them the investigation would be concluded that morning and the tracks would be cleared again by the end of the day.

Maya politely pulled out her press badge and with a smile requested permission to enter and shoot photos of the scene.

Realizing he was dealing with a legitimate photojournalist from America, Poval became even more hospitable, holding the tape up high for them to pass under and telling them to take a long as they needed.

Passing the perimeter tape, Maya began to take several photos of the scene with the piles of rusted car wrecks in the background, the morning mist still hanging in the air, drawing up images of an apocalyptic movie scene. Ken raise his cell phone and snapped some photos, looking over at her camera-back screen from time to time to notice just how much of a higher quality and better job she did of framing her shots. He stood back and admired as she took close-ups of the upside-down wheels, the rusted undercarriages, bent metal frames, shattered crate pieces, and scattered fresh oranges amongst the wreckage. She flitted around the wreck like a bee at a flower bed, her camera in constant motion.

Ken leaned around a container whose side had appeared to come off after it collided with another rolling stock and scraped down the berm to rest on its side. It had been loaded with large boxes of home furniture, several of which had split open in the crash, revealing dark wood cabinetry. He turned and saw Maya had taken photos of him inspecting the wreck. He smiled, and she snapped a few more.

"I hope you delete the ones of me smiling," he said, realizing it would look out of place at a train wreck.

She chuckled, "I'd have to have you sign a release if I wanted to use these for anything other than my own personal collection," she replied.

"Well, then I'm okay on you keeping them."

"Why, thank you," she replied with an earnest nod. "You're now a part of the whole narrative of my trip—the earthquake on the bridge and now this train wreck. My friends would tell me I invented you if I didn't have evidence. Who would believe I'd find a handsome American teacher in the wilds of the Tongariro Park?"

Ken found himself smiling at her compliment and she quickly stepped away to frame a shot with a bush filled with native flowers in the foreground. He realized she'd dropped a hint and stepped away before he could respond. A concern came over him that she might anticipate more than a friendship to come between them. He wondered how that conversation with her friends would play out and what emotions she had now subdued, that she would openly reveal to them.

As they made their way back to the officers, Ken said, "Well, I hope I'm not a sign of bad luck for you."

"Bad luck? Oh no, come one. Quite the opposite. I'm a photojournalist and incidents like these, unfortunate for some as they may be, are what we hope to find. Each time I've met you has been only good luck for me. I'm thinking I should stick with you for more."

Officer Poval seemed eager to engage the two foreign visitors in conversation, asking to see some of the photos she'd gotten and praising her skills as she showed him what she'd taken and explained how she will fix them up afterwards.

"Bet this is the most excitement you've had around here in a while?" Maya asked.

"Oh yes, for sure. We get the occasional car wrecks each year, but this is the first train wreck, and I've worked this region going on twenty years," Poval responded with an agreeing nod. He pronounced *first* as *furst*.

The other officer nodded at them and politely asked "You both from the States, aye?"

"Yes, we are," Ken replied. "She's on a photo assignment, and I'm just visiting relatives."

"Oh, sweet," he responded, appearing to lack the nerve to ask anything further.

Poval continued on with a nervous shuffle of his own. "This is probably nothing compared to what you see in the US I'll bet. But you watch, come back here in a couple hours, and this will become quite the attraction for the TV crews and locals. Everyone will want to come see," and he put quotations in the air, "'the train that ran off the tracks!' For us Kiwis, this will be headline news for a couple days. And you came down early to get the first shots. Good on you." He nodded effusively again.

"Yeah, I'm in town doing some photojournalism about the volcano here, and of course I couldn't pass this up," Maya responded.

"Oh, a journalist interested in our volcano?" he said with some mirth, becoming more garrulous. He looked to his taciturn partner for support and got none. "Well, do you know how this mountain got here?" he asked with a wink and another nervous shuffle.

Maya anticipated a trick question and motioned with her hands for him to continue, playing along with him, "Enlighten me Sir, please."

"Well you see, mountains are gods to the Maori. Aotearoa—their word for the islands we call New Zealand—was created by their ancestors, and the first thing to come out of the sea was the mountains and then the rest of the land. The mountains were not to be climbed or even looked at by the Maori because they were gods. Deeply respected," he added with a feigned bow. "They have maintained that respect for them for some two thousand years." He pronounced *years,* with *yeers*.

"Interesting," Ken said.

"Yeah," the officer continued. "But it gets better. The Gods have jealousies and marital issues just like us mortal folks, you see. This one here, a beautiful female when she's not hiding behind her veil," he said, motioning his arms to where the mountain would be behind the cloudy sky, "was once married to Taranaki, the big male, over to the east," he said, pointing. "But Tongariro over there to the north stole Ruapehu away. Taranaki and Tongariro had an epic battle during which Taranaki lost and was banished. But Ruapehu still loves Taranaki, and if I remember right, the eruptions and smoke sometimes coming from these volcanos has something to do with the anger, jealousy, and longing this threesome have unresolved."

He looked over to his partner for confirmation. The officer, who had been standing listening, gave a shy but knowing nod, "sounds right, Gov."

"This park with these mountains," Officer Poval continued with many elocutionary bobs of his head, "were gifted to the world by a Maori chief back in the late eighteen hundreds so that no one individual could lay claim to the mountains. This became the first national park in New Zealand and also one of the first in the world."

"Well, you two both must be proud to be serving the region," Ken acknowledged.

They nodded agreeably, and with their permission, Maya took photos of them with their oranges, the train, and car wrecks behind them.

After having them sign simple release documents she carried in her pocket, Maya and Ken thanked the proud officers for their time, returning up the gravel road.

CHAPTER SEVEN

Cynthia was already outside the cabin in a jacket, one leg up on a wooden fence that circled a paddock as she attempted with an outstretched arm to coax several alpacas to come to her. The animals kept a close distance, eyeing her with curiosity, approaching, and then jittering away.

As Ken and Maya came up the drive, she gave up on the animals and greeted them. Maya shared with her the photos she took and recounted the officer's manners and polite explanation of the park's Maori origins. They walked up into the main house where Ruth stood at the griddle in the kitchen. The smell of eggs and bacon wafted through the place.

"Good morning, everyone! Everyone sleep okay?" she said with a big smile in greeting. "Figured we'd do a traditional Kiwi fry-up for breakie, aye?"

They caught her up on the morning activities and sat down at the dining room table beside the open kitchen. Ken found himself consciously sitting close to Maya with a mix of allure and concern. He acknowledged to himself he was attracted to her free spirit and creative personality and that there was no harm in them becoming friends. She seemed like the kind of women that was in charge of her own life and didn't carry the baggage and drama he was used to. But he had also vowed to himself to ignore attractions for well into the next year so as to put enough of the past behind him and get himself into the right frame of mind to not repeat mistakes. She was making him second guess his decision.

Maya raised an eyebrow to Ken as she and Cynthia were served first, seeming to pick up his thoughts. He must have blushed at her, but she missed it, instead pointing to the fried tomatoes and made a questioning face.

Ken pointed to each thing on her plate: "Fried tomatoes, fried toast, eggs sunny side up, and bacon."

"I know what those are," she said with a smirk. "I've just never had fried tomatoes with my breakfast."

"You allergic to them?"

"No, I like tomatoes in sandwiches and salad."

Ken gave her a conspiratorial smile. "Then you'll really like them with your eggs and bacon. Dig in."

Ruth had the radio on as she cooked, tuned to a national broadcast in which a female did a steady monotone reading of the business news in a fluent New Zealand accent, covering a bulletin on the controversial raising of tariffs. Ruth gave a hush to the table as she came out of the kitchen and turned up the volume.

"...registered as a 3.9 tremor that shook the Tongariro National Park. No immediate structural damage was reported. A freight locomotive with no passengers derailed in Horopito later in the evening, southwest of Ruapehu. Investigators say there is a likely link between the earthquake that day with the evening's derailment, but no official statement of such has yet to be released. Officials continue to monitor Ruapehu, which has had an increase of daily tremors in recent months, but have said there is not a need to raise the threat level at this time. We will now go to Brad Mullinger for Sport..."

Ruth turned the radio down again and went back into the kitchen. She spoke loudly as she worked so the conversation could continue. "The GeoNet website this morning showed the increase of the activity, which I keep an eye on from time to time."

"Yeah, I was looking at that this morning too," Cynthia added.

Ruth put a glob of dark yellow butter on the grill, a satisfying sizzle rising up. "If you're really obsessed with the volcano, you can watch the 'Volcano Cam' link on the net which is a full-time camera at Crater Lake. Some enthusiasts like to watch it when the scientists bring their helicopters in over the lake, lowering a sample gathering container on a rope into it. But when the mountain lets off some smoke, everyone in town has their devices tuned to that link."

"Sounds like they monitor it pretty well," Maya observed.

"We do feel very safe by the mountain, really," Ruth said, cracking an egg. "Ruapehu has erupted every so many years, mostly just letting off some steam. The scientists that monitor the volcano measure earthquakes every day, most too small for us to feel. I meet some of them around town. Really nice people. About every couple decades it really erupts, and we might get a lahar and a plume of ash going up into the sky. But in the many years I've lived here, we've only been asked to evacuate this area once and were allowed to return in a couple days."

"What are lahars?" Ken asked, putting down his tea cup.

Ruth nodded at Cynthia to let the scientist answer.

Cynthia put her fingertips together in the shape of a volcano, "A lahar is like a mud flow that comes from a volcano. It might be a mix of water, ash, and rock that rapidly melted from ice and snow at the top or poured out of a crater lake." She pointed to where her fingers had met, "Ruapehu has a large lake in its crater at the top that will empty in a major eruption, and all that water has to have somewhere to go. It will slide down the mountain, carrying rocks and trees with it, tearing up the land." She used her fingers around her imaginary volcano to show the stream of sliding destruction. "Most people think of lava and ash as the main destruction a volcano creates, but lahars can be just as dangerous, if not more, as they are more sudden and move faster." She looked up at Ruth, who nodded approvingly.

Ruth pointed her spatula for effect, "The largest volcanic disaster in New Zealand's history occurred right here with Ruapehu in 1953, well before I was born, in case you were wondering," she added with a wink. "It traveled down the mountain during the night and took out a bridge just minutes before a train of sleeping passengers plunged off it to their death." She raised her eyebrows for effect, looking around at each of her guests.

"Aren't you pretty far from any damage the volcano could cause?" Ken asked with concern.

Ruth shrugged, bringing plates of breakfast for Ken and her and sitting down to eat. "Yeah, no lahar should come near here they say. But you never really can think you are assured nothing will happen. That's why I park rear-first in my drive—easier to get out in a hurry. Floridians have about a once in a hundred year chance of their home being damaged in a hurricane, and a Californian in the countryside has about a once in a hundred year chance of his being destroyed by fire. The good thing about this threat is science has gotten so good; with the last lahar in '07, they were able to warn of it coming and predict its exact breaking point from the top and its path down the mountain. We had a torrent of mud coming down like a river, but all on a predicted path, and no one was injured."

After a pause to chew and swallow, she continued, "I find there is something else to living here in such a beautiful setting. It seems the people that share this place—the couple thousand there are between the few small towns and hamlets around the mountain, like this Horopito here—seem to share a sense of community that goes beyond the 'love thy neighbor' and more to a 'love, protect and look out for thy neighbor.' Everyone has a sixth sense of what the mountain is doing and shows it utmost respect. It is like the sailor who has to constantly be aware of and respect the threat of the ocean. But if he follows the rules of the ocean, he can eat from it, travel on it, and benefit from all its splendor."

Cynthia who had been writing furiously in her notebook, looked up with a smile, "I knew we'd come to the right house."

"Well, my publicist will want royalties on any quote you publish," Ruth replied with a chuckle.

They all laughed until Ruth's cell came to life, and she looked down at it, fumbling with her earbuds to take the call. "Hello Brodie," she said. She listened, eyes staring ahead at nothing for a minute, and then a frown came across her face. She got up from the table with her phone and walked into the kitchen. Ken could hear only her acknowledging what Brodie was saying and then her describing the train wreck down the road, blocking the exit. Ken turned his attention back to Cynthia and Maya, and they got to discussing the various Maori carvings adorning the walls of the house and the paintings of local birds and made comments on the many differences between the States and New Zealand, some subtle and some glaring.

CHAPTER EIGHT

Ruth came back to the table after some minutes, her mood having changed. "That was one of my employees," she said, sitting back down. "He has to go to an emergency hui with his Maori tribe tomorrow and is asking permission to not come to work." She saw Maya's questioning frown and explained that a hui was a Maori tribal meeting.

"The local elders want to address concerns over the mountain. I have no idea what they think they are going to do. This happens about once a year and usually means a lot of talk and speculation and then more of nothing. Brodie's new girlfriend happens to be an interning scientist at GeoNet, which monitors the tectonic plates around here. He feels it's important they attend to address the concerns from a scientific basis and less spiritual or superstitious. And to top it off, he also reports complaints with one of our tenants which I will have to go see myself and handle." She shook her head, taking another bite from her eggs.

"I'd love to be able to observe this Maori meeting about the mountain," said Cynthia. "Do you think they'd let me? It would add color to our story."

Ruth swallowed her bite and shrugged, "I could text Brodie back and tell him who you are and ask him to get permission to bring you along. I don't think they'd object."

That afternoon the temperature had risen to where they could shed their jackets, and they decided to take a walk down to the wreck site. As predicted, it was now accompanied by repair crews, a news van, and a small crowds of spectators. A crane was being used to lift each rolling stock onto flatbed trucks to drive them away. They waved to Officer Poval and his partner, joined the rubbernecking for a little while, and quickly got bored with it.

Ruth took them for a walk further down the road, pointing out local flora and regaling them with stories of the local history from the pioneer days. She told them about her grandmother who was a midwife in the original construction camps that first tamed the land at the turn of the nineteenth century, building the railroads and viaducts through the region, linking the northern cities to the capital at the south. They stopped to watch a fantail flit through the air, hunting insects.

As they turned to walk back to the house, Ken stopped in his tracks and pointed. "There she is!" he exclaimed. They followed his gaze up to see sections of the cloud layer had moved aside exposing the mountain to view for the first time, like a theatre curtain opening to a grandly lit stage. The behemoth rose up, high on the horizon. The top was a long flat shape of jagged teeth covered in snow and rocky outcroppings. Compared to other typical volcanos in the North Island with their symmetrical cone shapes, this was the aged and stooped veteran, evidence of its past eruptions and volatile nature.

They stood and stared up at it in awe. "Amazing to think something so huge sits there, the whole time concealed," said Ken with a shake of his head.

"Yeah, the mountain creates its own weather system," Cynthia explained. "It can be cool and pleasant down here but just half an hour drive up you might encounter light rain and then an hour up near the top there might be a snowstorm."

Maya stepped back and took photos of them looking up at the mountain.

As they walked back Ruth took another call from Brodie, listening to him for a minute and then said, "Hold on Brodie, I'm going to put you on speaker and have you repeat that to my nephew and a couple American friends we've just met." She tapped her phone and held it out between everyone.

"*Kia Ora everyone! So, yeah, just telling Ruth that, um, my lady-friend tells me the alert level for Ruapehu is about to be raised to two, which kinda means they think there might be some small chance of the lady lighting her pipe, you know? But we've seen this before, haven't we Ruth?*" Ruth gave a knowing nod. "*Most the time she keeps her temper in check. I don't think we've got much to get our knickers in a twist about.*" With his strong accent he sounded jovial and relaxed, pleased to give them the inside scoop.

"Did you see my text about Cynthia being able to attend your hui tomorrow?" Ruth asked.

"Ah yea, that's cool. I told my uncle, and he grunted. Not something fancy."

They made arrangements to meet the next day and hung up the call. Ruth's daughter and grandkids were planning on driving down from Auckland in the morning, and after calling her and talking about the alert level change, they decided after Ruth had taken care of some chateau rental business concerns, Ruth and Ken will instead drive up to Auckland and spend time with them there.

That evening it was Cynthia and Maya's turn to tell them about their past adventures and planned travels around the Ring of Fire to capture how people have adapted to living with volcanos. The conversation flowed through dinner on the porch as the day had continued to warm and the sky had entirely cleared, allowing the setting sun to bask the mountain in an orange hue. Ruth held court over the conversation, eliciting stories of awkward, astonishing, and embarrassing moments from both of them which brought out gasps and fits of laughter. She also filled them with suggestions of things to catch in their travels through the country.

During the evening Ken and Maya exchanged several awkward glances and coy smiles. When talking about her experiences and past travels, she seemed to be talking for his benefit to give him a sense of who she was and how she conducted her life.

Darkness had arrived by the time the wine bottle was empty. The conversation continued as they washed up the dishes and mingled around the living room, each wishing the evening didn't have to end.

Cynthia broke the spell with a look at her watch, a reluctant shake of the head and comment how they would have to rise early to head out in the morning. They donned their jackets, and Ken offered to walk Cynthia and Maya to their cabin.

They stepped out onto the lawn in the cool air and black of night with the light of their phones to guide them. Maya craned her head up. "Oh. My. Gawd!" she exclaimed.

With the clouds now gone, above them the Milky Way and thousands of bright stars painted the night sky in a stunning display of vivid colors and sparkles. The three of them stood there for a moment, each feeling suddenly small and insignificant before the immensity of the galaxy above them.

"Look, there's the Southern Cross," Ken said, pointing out the famous constellation only seen below the equator. "And there's Jupiter and that bright guy there is Saturn. Oh my, there are so many amazing things you can see from here," he said trailing off.

"You an astronomer?" Maya asked.

"No, just enjoy it as a hobby," Ken responded. They stared up at the night sky for several moments, taking in the stark band of varied light that is the Milky Way and the vivid colors and bright pin pricks scattered across the sky like diamonds against a black cloth. "See that small but bright collection of stars all gathered together there, looking like one ball of light?" he said pointing. They acknowledged him. "That's called Omega Centauri, around twenty thousand light-years away and is the largest-known globular cluster in the Milky Way. In that little ball there are something like ten million stars."

"Damn. I've got to get some shots of this," Maya decided suddenly. "Help me get my equipment, will you?" she said to Ken, heading to the cabin.

"Well, you two eat your heart out. I'm going to bed," Cynthia replied, following after them.

They entered the wood cabin, which looked like it had been built several decades ago in a rustic unvarnished style without any upgrades or changes. Maya headed over to her equipment cases and luggage, which had been arranged on a bare wood dining table in the middle of the main room. A few doors going into bedrooms and bunk rooms completed the place. Brass pots and pans covered the walls of the open kitchen with ceramic bowls and plates lining the wainscoting that stretched across the wall. A bulbous cathode-ray TV from years past sat in the corner, fronted by old couches of questionable comfort. Maya pulled out a tripod from a hard case and began selecting various lenses and cameras.

Ken stepped over and admired the array of options. His picked up the strap attached to one of the cameras, admiring its black nylon material with *National Geographic Society* stitched in bold yellow letters down it. "This is really nice," he said.

She looked over and smiled. "Here," she said, rummaging in a suitcase of clothes, "have one." She pulled out a spare strap and tossed it to him. He caught it. "Wow, thank you," he said, testing its elasticity. "If I put this on my little point-and-shoot will I look like a poser?" he asked humorously.

She tittered, "Every photographer starts somewhere."

They went outside and onto the lawn away from the house where the least light could distract the view. Their eyes adjusted quickly as they refocused on the light coming from the stars. Maya opened her large tripod and began assembling the equipment, mounting her Nikon. Ken watched as she rapidly pushed buttons and adjusted various settings on the camera display, testing positions and views. She was confident and at ease. She turned on an iPad, putting it on dark-light settings, and in a few minutes, the camera began streaming photos to it, which she then shared with Ken. She tried various wide-angle images that included the skyline, playing with settings and lamenting not having a motorized mount that would track the Earth's motion with the camera.

The images, taken even with short exposures, looked stunning. Ken tried to take some of the same frames with his iPhone and looked with dismay at the result. "Can you give me some of those too?" he asked.

"Sure," she replied, taking his phone from him. She synced the camera with it and sent several shots to him.

She confirmed they appeared in his photo library and handed it back to him. "I don't see any photos of your girlfriend," she commented with a half-smile, looking at the shadow of his face in the dark.

The comment hung heavy in the air, and it took Ken a moment to register its full intent.
His response seemed to come from an even darker place. "She's living with another man." The hurt was visible, even in the darkness.

"Oh, sorry," Maya replied, realizing she'd touched a fresh wound.

"That's okay," Ken said, looking out at the skyline. "That's the main reason I came here. I needed some time and space away from it all."

Maya felt her heart go out to him, wanting to do something that would take away the pain but knew there was hardly a role she could play in easing his loss. She might only be a reminder and likely make things worse if she reached for him. "I know the feeling," she said softly. She turned away and put the lens cap on. "I've lived on the road nine months of the year, and the couple stable relationships I thought I had didn't last." She nervously stole a glance back at him. "I've found men aren't really looking for an internet girlfriend." She began to collapse the tripod.

Ken nodded to himself, his heart and mind whirling, unable to come up with a good reply. How could he fall for a women he met in a foreign country who was practically a stranger that lived on the road and in a different part of his state? He felt if he backed away and said goodbye he would save his already broken heart from further damage.

"I'm sure the right person will come along. You deserve it," he said softly.

She mumbled a half-hearted thank you and picked up her camera bag and tripod. Instinctively she stepped over to him, reached up and pecked him on the cheek, hardly aware she was doing it. "Good night."

CHAPTER NINE

Ken lay in his bed, his cheek flush and tingling as he replayed the simple act of a kiss on the cheek over and over in his mind. The next morning they would be saying goodbye and returning to what was their normal life. He debated with himself the ethics of pursuing a relationship that might upend either or both of their lives. He thought about how they could both flourish together, fantasizing fantastical future scenarios. He felt the stressful anguish relationships cause, but in this case, he realized there was truth to the honest emotions that he felt. Around her he felt open, happy, and fulfilled in some unusual way he was not used to. He argued with himself about the rights and wrongs in pursuing something with her. Unable to sleep, he got up from his bed and found a Chateau Rentals notepad in a desk drawer in the room and began to write.

Maya paced the main room of the cabin in her pajamas, running her hand through her hair, putting it up, and letting it fall repeatedly as she fought her own internal emotions. She thought she should feel ashamed for flirting with Ken and coming onto him, but for some reason she didn't. She instead felt sorrow for him and in a way helpless at being unable to make him see her as a possible solution for his problems. She thought about having to leave the next morning, being around Ruth and Cynthia the whole time, and not having a last chance to speak to him in private or leave an impression with him that will make him respond to her. She tried to analytically assess her emotions, asking herself if she was sincere in her feelings for him and not acting irrational or hasty. She knew she couldn't possibly assure herself she was correct, but had to act on her gut instinct. She tore a page from her work journal and began to write.

The next morning Ken insisted on helping Ruth cook breakfast for all of them, mostly so he would not have to endure the awkward conversation with Maya as they avoided talking about what was really on both their minds. He had to do something to avoid his desire to stare at her and engage her in a long and deep conversation that would reveal how he felt about her.

After they arrived for breakfast, Maya played the same part, remaining engrossed with her phone and in coordination with Cynthia about their project's future planning. She hardly glanced at Ken when he joined them at the table to eat, which he found irritating. Ruth plied them with further questions about their work and future plans, but it was clear everyone was thinking ahead to saying goodbye and moving on with the day.

Ken forced himself to eat his food and drink his tea in silence, his appetite waning as the minutes passed. He wondered if she was able to so simply ignore him and shut him out of her life now that he had told her his real reason for being there.

Then, when the other two women were looking away in a discussion of an old map of the Ruapehu region on the wall beside the dining room, Maya turned to him and gave a warm knowing smile and a sigh, and he unconsciously responded in kind, feeling his heart surge in relief.

He felt that if in just a few days she had this much of an effect on him, he would have to obey his heart, not his mind, or fear losing his sanity.

Half an hour later they were at their rental car, their bags loaded. They had exchanged cell phone and contact info and promised to stay in touch and ephemeral plans of maybe they could get together again when they next visited the other's country. Ruth gave Cynthia and Maya each a hug.

After a cordial hug with Cynthia, Ken turned to Maya and felt an emotional surge well up inside him. He realized their connection had been entirely platonic with little physical contact, until this simple hug goodbye. They embraced, and he felt her squeeze him tightly, whispering a thank you for everything in his ear. Pulling back, he saw her eyes had teared up, and she apologized, wiping the tears away with a polished index finger. Taking her left hand in his, he spoke quietly to her, "Let's stay in comm, okay?"

She nodded effusively. "Yes, please. I would like that." She reached into her back pocket and pulled out a piece of paper just as Ken was reaching into his back pocket and pulling out a small envelope. They giggled as they handed each other the papers, knowing they must contain communication neither could say in words, but could only be said in writing.

She beamed and reached up to him, kissing him on the cheek again before getting into the car as Cynthia drove them away.

Ken and Ruth stood there and waved as they turned out of sight. Neither said anything for a moment. Ruth looked over at him and nodded at the paper he held in his hand. "You going to let that one get away?" she asked with an eyebrow raise and a smile.

In the car Cynthia looked across at the smile on Maya's face and the envelope in her hand. "That's a guy worth holding onto; you know that, right?"

Maya sighed deeply and nodded in agreement. She opened the envelope and read Ken's message:

"Maya, This is very hard for me to write, but my mind keeps turning and I can't sleep. I feel I must write this down in knowing I can communicate more   clearly through paper than in person. I came here to my family in New Zealand to get away from the misery and depression I was feeling after my marriage had fallen apart. Prior to meeting you on that bridge, inside I was an emotional mess. I realized tonight that since the earthquake we shared, none of that has mattered. It is like you somehow shook it out of me. I have looked forward to being around you and enjoyed every minute of my time with you. This is the healing I was looking for. You did this just by being you. You haven't had

the chance to really tell me how you feel, but I know you have made clear you are interested in at least finding out. I would be a fool to pass you by. Let us stay connected and find a way to come together when you are back in California, even if just to see if this was real or a dream. Love, Ken"

CHAPTER TEN

"When they open the door, you just stand there and let me talk to them," Ruth told Ken, who was holding Sabre on his leash. They had arrived at a home on the edge of Ohakune, the small town at the base of the mountain that acted as a ski village, its few main roads providing some restaurants and hotels for the out-of-towners that come to have fun on the mountain. The house was a bungalow enclosed by trees with a wide front porch, lying beside the Mangawhero River that came down from the mountain. A blue windowless van was parked beside the house. All the windows of the home were closed but they could hear voices and feel the motion of bodies through the floorboards. "Let me talk to them. We've already had several neighbor complaints about these tenants, and they aren't going to be pleased to be told they have to leave. Brodie would normally accompany me for visits like this, and so I want you here, just in case." Ruth knocked loudly and stepped back.

Ken was going to ask, "just in case of what?" when an antagonistic Russian accent came through the unopened door. "Who there?"

"Hello, this is Ruth Sybil, the owner of Chateau Rentals," she said loudly in a professional tone, speaking through the door. "I wish to speak to you about the cancellation of your rental agreement."

The door was cracked open, and a tall Russian man showed his face. He was well over six feet with short graying hair and a stubble beard. He looked at her, annoyed. "We have no problem. We are paid."

"I'm sorry but we are going to have to cancel the agreement after several complaints we have received which violate the conditions of the contract." Ken was surprised by how calmly she said this, like she had rehearsed and delivered the lines many times before.

The door opened a little further, and he put his whole body in the frame, deliberately seeking to impose on her with his physical presence. "You don't know who you mess with," he replied with a sneer.

"Mr…" she looked down at the papers in her hand "…Kise—le—vich, you don't get to refuse this order. It will be enforced by local authorities if needed."

He let out a little guttural laugh. "Local authorities? I see what authorities. They wimps."

Ruth seemed to hesitate, unsure what tact to take with this man. Ken looked at her, worried. The man had a threatening presence, and pushing him could result in more trouble than they would want. "Then I will inspect the premises now and we

can talk further. No need to let us in the front door;
I have the keys to the back."

This seemed to catch him by surprise. "No,
you not inspect." he said, with a sudden urgent
tone.

"Do I need to detail for you each of the
complaints of loud noises and rude behavior
during normal neighborhood quiet hours?"

"We fix this."

"Yes, you were given the chance to do so,
and still we receive more complaints."

"You not coming in and we not leaving," he
said, defiant again.

Out of the corner of her eye Ruth saw Ken
bend down, whisper something, and unleash
Sabre. The dog shot off, head down, sniffing along
the front of the porch. It scampered down the
steps and began moving around the house,
heading toward the van.

"No! Call back dog! No! all right! We leave
this morning. We go." He had opened the door
wide and was nodding at Ruth, suddenly contrite.
Two other men had come to the entrance, both
clearly Russian with worried looks on their faces.
They began to talk to each other in heavy accents,
gesticulating. They looked over at the dog, moving
rapidly along the front of the house. Ken had no
idea what they were saying to each other, but their
voices rapidly became shouting and what must
have been cursing as they accused the larger man
of somehow betraying them.

"Today, gentlemen. Today!" Ruth said,
walking off the porch with Ken. They looked over
where Sabre had gone and saw the dog was
excitedly circling the van, looking for a way in,
quietly growling.

"Sabre!" Ruth shouted. The dog froze in place, looking back at her. "Heel boy!" she commanded.

The dog looked back at the van, seeming to hesitate, and then ran over to them, leaping into the Land Rover as the door was opened. The Russians watched them pull out, one of them throwing his arms in the air in frustration at the tall guy while the other ran around to the back of the house.

"That was really strange behavior. Definitely need to report them. They are not here on a ski trip," Ruth said. "What do you think Sabre was doing?" she asked.

Sabre had squeezed himself between the two front seats, seeking attention. Ken turned around and began to scratch him behind the ears. In a silly voice he replied, "Sabre was hunting rabbits, wasn't he? Weren't you, Sabre?"

Ruth cackled, "Good doggie!"

CHAPTER ELEVEN

Ten minutes later they were heading back down a long empty country road with green hilly pastures on either side. Flocks of sheep appeared as tufts of white, scattered on the landscape, methodically grazing. The sun was bright, and a cool breeze had come in. Ruth flashed her lights and began to slow the vehicle. Ahead of her a pickup truck flashed its lights and too began to slow. The vehicles came to a stop beside each other in the middle of the road. Both windows came down, and Ruth said, "Hey Brodie!"

Brodie beamed and nodded at Ruth. "Kia Ora, Bro!" he said with a wave at Ken, like he was greeting an old friend. A young Maori lady in a polo shirt with a logo on her chest sat in the passenger seat, smiling. Brodie's heavyset frame filled the entire front seat of his pickup. His long black hair was in a ponytail making the tattoos visible up the side of his neck. Ken waved from his seat, and Sabre let out a bark. "This is Kayana," he said to

Ken, motioning to his lady-friend. She waved a hello.

Brodie continued on like they were at a cafe, resting his sizable arm out the window. "The hui was all good, yeah. Your friends, they were great. Answered questions and even talked to the elders, showing respect. Kayana," he said, looking back at her, "she did this whole whiteboard thing and showed all the sites where tremors have been in the past couple days. Damn lot of them, aye?" The girl beside him gave an embarrassed chuckle.

"She says it's a bit more than normal. Brought along a container of murky and smelly sulphuric water that was taken from Crater Lake at the top with their helicopter couple days ago. Nice 'show and tell' aye? We all got to have a sniff!" He chuckled at his humor. "The lake is over one hundred degrees now. Hot stuff! Could make a good cuppa. My uncle and them, they did some prayers and all that. All good."

Ruth and Ken nodded with him, and then Ruth told him the troubled tenants will be out that day and he can send the cleaners in to prepare it for the next renters. As she was telling him they'd be back from Auckland in a week, a car appeared in the distance, coming in their direction. They quickly said their goodbyes and pulled away from each other.

"He's a good man, that Brodie," Ruth said as she sped up. "Known him since he was little and would come with his dad to do work around our home on the weekend for extra cash. Had big dreams of playing rugby professionally and becoming an All Black. But some injuries held him back, plus an incident with some mates at a roadside bar resulted in two men hospitalized, and

Brodie got charged. He got cut from the team after that. Then his girl left him, which I consider was a good thing, given how he wouldn't have been with that crowd if he hadn't been with her. He was a blubbering mess for weeks. I picked him up, put him to work, and demanded he get his life in order. He treats me like I'm his mum now. His actual mum doesn't seem to care what happens to him, so he comes to me for life advice and such."

After a lunch of mince pies in a cafe by her place of work in town, they headed back to her lodge to pack their bags for the drive north to the big city. Ken felt the strange pang of loneliness with Maya no longer around. She and Cynthia had said they planned to extend their stay around the mountain for several more days, excited for the opportunity to document the changes happening and how the town responds. As he packed his bags Ken pulled out Maya's note and read her neat handwriting for the fifth time that day:

"Ken, I know we did not mean to run into each other like this and you came here to heal as you say, not regrow. Well, maybe fate has a funny way of guiding people's lives. I just would be remiss and possibly regret it for the rest of my life if I did not tell you how I really feel and let you know that once you are done with your time healing and ready to let another into your life again, I am hoping I can be an easy choice you can make. I will complete this Ring of Fire assignment in a month or so and be back in California with time to myself. This might coincide with your next school break. Maybe not. In either case, you've stolen my heart with your

humility, honestly and intelligence. I don't know how to explain it, but something in my heart tells me to say this. ML, Maya"

CHAPTER TWELVE

Ruth and Ken drove north for a couple hours through Tongariro National Park, the road a straight two-lane highway that took them through kilometer after kilometer of flat, shrub-filled terrain with Mount Tgauruhoe and then Mount Tongariro far to their right, the two other large volcanic mountains in the park. As they exited the park and drove the highway road north, the peaks slowly receded in the rear.

They arrived at Lake Taupo where the road continued for half an hour along a scenic route, circling the lake that filled their view on the left. They eventually arrived into the town of Taupo at the north end of the lake where they planned to eat and rest for the night. They checked into a hotel on the lakefront, and Ken took Sabre for a late afternoon walk on the beach along the lakefront.

The wind had picked up, tugging on Ken's jacket and sending spindrift into the air from the small breakers. Waves lapped the shoreline and pulled at bits of driftwood. Sabre pulled along, eager for the exercise. Ken looked out across the water and could see a few sailboats in the far distance, close to the opposite shore. The southern shoreline was invisible, being so far away and obscured by haze. Seeing no one else around, he let Sabre off the leash and watched him playfully race across the beach. Ken slowed his walk and breathed in deep, trying to settle his mind. He reminded himself he'd come here to find relaxation and get away from mental pain that had been burned in him by the opposite sex. This had been working, but here he was feeling the fire reignited again. And once again, he felt unsure of his confidence in making a firm decision, whether he should be pursuing or ignoring.

Ken reached down and picked up some of the rocks that lined the shoreline. They were all a light pumice. He threw some out into the water, watching them splash into the small waves, and then selected some whose shapes would be good to take home to his sister for an exfoliating bath.

When they returned to the hotel Ken showed Ruth the pumice stones he'd picked up and commented how this was the first time he'd seen stones like this on a beach.

"You're not looking at a normal beach," she said with mirth. "That's a caldera, what is left of the volcano that once sat there." Ken raised his eyebrows. "Yep, entire lake was formed by a volcanic explosion some thousands of years ago. Sent ash into the air that supposedly darkened the sky and cooled the temperature of the entire planet. Reportedly ancient Chinese writings recorded the changes in the atmosphere caused by the explosion, and evidence can be seen in earth sediment layers all around the world. That pumice you are holding is rock that had air forced through it at such high temperatures it creates those tiny holes you see." She nodded and raised her eyebrows at him, showing off her knowledge of the local geology. "If you wish to know any more you'll have to ask someone like Cynthia, because that's about where my intellect ends," she said with a laugh.

Ken looked out the hotel window at the huge lake beyond, trying to imagine it all being regular land or something like Ruapehu standing there and in an instant being blown into the sky with an indescribable force of nature.

CHAPTER THIRTEEN

"**O**h, Cynthia will be excited about that," Ruth said, pointing at the TV mounted in the corner of the small cafe. They were eating an early morning eggs, toast, and tea breakfast before heading out for the last leg of their trip to Auckland. On the screen was a live image of Ruapehu with a single trail of smoke coming out the top, like a kettle giving off steam. The announcer was reporting on the alert level having been raised to "Two" the day before and might be raised to "Three" if the volcano shows further signs of continuing buildup. She commented how authorities saw no signs of imminent danger to homes or life, though the ski fields were being ordered to close as a precaution. The screen changed to a view of the single road coming down the mountain with several cars loaded with skis and snowboards atop them. A local resident was quoted on camera saying, "Well, something's upset the lady, and she's just letting off some steam. These things happen."

Ken sent Maya his first text: *Looks like you and Cynthia are getting what you came for*, with a smiley emoji. His phone indicated it was delivered, but no indicator came it was read, and after several minutes there was no reply. He felt introverted and wondered if there was something wrong with what he said that he wasn't seeing.

Leaving the cafe, Ken looked into the distance to where Ruapehu would be but saw only fleecy clouds. He reminded himself there were two other volcanic mountains between Lake Taupo and Ruapehu and he couldn't see those either. He told himself to let these thoughts about Maya and the mountain go and move on with his trip and find the new normal in his life that he was seeking. He turned away and got into the Land Rover.

Half an hour into the drive, passing through thick forests of planted evergreen trees, Ruth's cell phone came to life with a call from Cynthia. She put it on speaker.

"Hi Cynthia, how you liking the mountain view now?" Ruth asked cheerfully.

"Oh, it's amazing. I'm going to be going up in a helicopter this afternoon to get a look into the Crater Lake." Her tone darkened. "But have you heard from Maya at all?"

Ruth looked at Ken, and he looked down at his phone, showing nothing received. He shook his head. "No," she replied, "She's not with you?"

"We split up yesterday after the tribal meeting. She went up the mountain to capture images of the lahar paths from the past and I stayed here to visit with the GeoNet scientists. We were to meet for dinner but she never returned and did not show at the hotel last night. I've been calling and texting her but getting no answer."

"Oh my gosh," Ruth said, worry in her voice.

"I've called the local police and they know nothing and they're not too helpful now that they are doing this whole evacuation of the ski areas." Desperation was in her voice. "I'm pretty sure she wouldn't be up at snow level as that's not where she would be shooting. If she got lost it wouldn't take that long to find her way back even if she walked all the way down. They want me to turn in a missing person report and I'm going to go do that. I called you in case she may have shown up at your house or something like that, but I don't know. I'm just desperate, worried she may have hurt herself somehow."

Ruth put her hand to her mouth in alarm, "Dearest, Ken and I left last night and stayed at a hotel in Taupo and are now a few hours north of you. I can call right now and have someone go over and check my home."

"Oh, okay, thank you." Cynthia sounded lost and distracted, seeing she had little else to go on. "I'm going to the station to do that missing person report and look again in all the places I can, show photos around and see the Park Rangers. I can't miss my helicopter reservation this afternoon though. I'll have my phone on me, so if you hear anything please call me right away."

"Absolutely, we will. I'm sure she's going to show up or be found soon," Ruth said.

After they hung up they drove in silence for a minute, both thinking about Maya and the significance of what they'd heard. Ken felt a shudder of anxiety. They glanced at each other and simultaneously asked, "Should we turn around?"

CHAPTER FOURTEEN

Half an hour later, as they were passing through Taupo again, Brodie called them back reporting no one was at the house or cabin. They asked him to meet them at her office when they arrive in two hours. As they drove they kept track of the activities around Mount Ruapehu through the GeoNet site and social media. A missing photojournalist was reported on the Ohakune police website, and the Park Rangers were alerted to be on the lookout for her. Nothing indicated an actual hunt for her was underway.

As they came into Tongariro National Park they could begin to see the thin plume above Mount Ruapehu on the horizon. It had visibly grown since the morning and had begun to flatten out with the cirrus clouds.

They called Cynthia who was at the airfield preparing to go up. When they told her they had turned around and would be back in an hour, she wept with tears of thanks. She told them she would be making a couple trips up to see the mountain and would be using her view from the helicopter to look for her too. They agreed to meet later in the day and told her she was welcome to stay with them again that night.

As the vehicle traveled the flat highway around Ruapehu they admired the trail of smoke rising steadily from its crater and saw helicopters hovering as tiny specks, documenting it from up high. Ken viewed some of the footage from the helicopters on his phone which showed where the plume originated from just above the edge of the crater lake, which remained in place, unchanged.

Ruth's place of business occupied a small blue building on the edge of town. A large painted sign announced "Chateau Rentals" with the outline of the serrated mountain behind the lettering. Brodie met them at the door, and Ken again was impressed by his gregariousness and size.

He told them he'd been over to the police station only to find the receptionist, Jasmine, overwhelmed with calls about the mountain plume. She had received and posted the missing person report on-line, but nothing further had been done. The few officers in town were busy directing traffic on the mountain evacuation. Additional officers were en route from surrounding towns, but would not be there for some hours. Everyone's attention was on the mountain. Jasmine had assured him if the photojournalist wasn't heard from by nightfall, they would assemble a search party.

Cynthia had told them she could be somewhere along the path of the last 2007 lahar. As large as that path was, they decided they could at least do a preliminary search to be doing something.

Ruth instructed Ken to take Brodie and Sabre in her Land Rover and go up the mountain while she went over to the police station in Brodie's truck and see what could be done further from there.

They grabbed some snacks and water bottles to bring with them and headed out to the parking lot. "Well Bro, shall we do this?" Brodie asked Ken with a toothy smile as they stood beside the vehicle.

Ken looked him up and down. "Isn't it cold up there? You ready to go like that?"

"Oh, yeah, good point." He ran back into the office and emerged with a grey hoodie on and a backpack.

"And your feet? You gonna be okay in sandals?"

Brodie looked down at his feet. "Sandals? These are jandals, Bro. Yeah, if we have to climb through the brush, I might take 'em off."

Ken raised his eyebrows and chuckled. "Okay, let's go. You guide."

They got in the vehicle, and Ken mentally reminded himself he was in New Zealand and had to drive on the left-side of the road. They passed a few blocks of restaurants and businesses renting snow gear or selling real estate and were on the single road leading up the mountain. Houses lined the sides for the first couple kilometers, and then they were driving beside a mountain river that was flowing strong. Ken was reminded of the trip he had made just two years earlier, carrying his mother's ashes back to her homeland. They had performed a small ceremony and scattered them in the eddies at the river's edge where he was passing now. He thought about the history his family had with this mountain and wondered what the next chapter they were writing now would bring.

The incline steepened as they drove through thick forested terrain. Both of them scanned the sides of the road, but could see little through the trees, rushes, ferns and vines, which let in little light. Ahead they arrived at a checkpoint where they were stopped by a police officer. Ken noticed it was the same one he and Maya had talked to at the train wreck.

"Hey Brodie," Officer Poval said.

"Good day to you, Squire," Brodie said with an affected British accent.

Poval placed his hands behind his back, bending down to see them both, and took on a mock tone of authority, "Well gentlemen, I'm sorry to say the road to the ski field has been closed."

"Me and my Bro here are just going to look around the lower ranges for that photographer that went missing yesterday."

"Oh yes, there was a radio call about that," he said with some concern. "I remember her."

"Nothing's been reported?" Ken asked.

"No, no sign of the young lady," he replied.

"Well, we'll just drive around a bit and look around, you know, see what we see and come back, aye?" Brodie said.

"Right-o gentlemen. Good luck." He tapped the vehicle, and they drove on.

"Poval and I have history," Brodie said with a chuckle. "He arrested me a few times in my youth. I deserved it too!" He laughed at the memory of his earlier self.

As they drove on, Ken kept looking off into the thick vegetation that reminded him of an Amazonian rainforest, expecting to see something and not wanting to miss anything. After a few minutes Brodie spoke up in a calming voice, "Mate, eye on the road. There's no chance we're going to see something through this bush at this level. Let's get higher where it thins out, and we'll be able to look around more and see what she was likely to be seeing."

Ken nodded in agreement, "You know this mountain well?"

"Oh yeah Mate, she's been home all my life. I grew up on this mountain. Only been working for Ruth for a few years now. She's part of my whānau —family, you know. Just glad I can be of help."

Ken nodded, worry on his face. They had been driving for ten minutes with nothing but thick vegetation on either side of the road, dropping his hopes further and making their task seem impossible.

"So where do you live in the States, Bro?" Brodie asked, trying to lighten the mood.

"San Diego," Ken replied.

"You see the Lakers?" Brodie was beaming.

"Yeah, I've been to some Laker games."

"No way! Oh man, I'd love to see the Lakers. They're my team, you know? Wish I could have seen Kobe. He was so flash."

Ken smiled and modestly said, "I saw Kobe play a few times."

"Get out Bro! I follow the NFL too. My team is the Jets."

"Jets? Why the Jets?" Ken asked with puzzlement as he slowed the vehicle to look over an opening in the terrain.

"I dunno. It's New York I guess."

"That team loses every year and hasn't been to the Super Bowl in half a century."

"Yeah, I know. The name stands for 'Just Endure The Suffering,' and I'm doing just that with them. One day though, one day, they'll make me happy for believing in them, and it will all be worth it."

Ken looked over at him and laughed. "You ever leave this country?"

"I've been up to the big city a few times, aye. Been to Eden Park."

"But you've never left the island?" Ken asked incredulously.

"No Mate, never," he said humbly. "Got to do my big OE someday. You know, the Overseas Experience. Been saving up for it. One day. I want to see where Kobe played and eat an In-'n-Out hamburger. I hear they put McDonald's to shame."

"Well, when you come over, look me up, and I'll take you to a Laker game, and you can have your hamburger."

"Oh, you're on Mate," he said, shifting excitedly in his chair.

"You never feel the need to move away?" Ken asked.

"This is my home. My tribe, Ngati Rangi, is here. All the people I know and I love are here. Why move away and leave them? That seems wrong, aye?"

Ken nodded, accelerating out of a sharp turn.

"You see, Maoris don't look at the world as you Americans do. It's like, I think the American— he's never satisfied and always looking for more, because his goal is sometimes money or fame or whatever the latest fashion is. He doesn't know how to be happy with what he's got, aye? We can be happy with just the sun and a beer, you know?"

Ken laughed at this and nodded his head.

"In Maori," Brodie continued, "our town 'Ohakune' means an 'an opening to a new world'. That's this little place. A new world!" he put his hands in the air with a flourish.

The conversation went on until the terrain noticeably changed with the road making a steeper incline and the foliage going from rainforest to tall thick Birch and then to shorter evergreens. "After the next corner there'll be a turn-off," Brodie said. "We should take it. It will give us a good view of the lahar fields on the western slope."

CHAPTER FIFTEEN

They took the sightseeing turn-off, parked, and got out of the car with Sabre on his leash. It was noticeably chillier with a strong breeze. Ken donned a zip-up jacket. Brodie pulled binoculars out of his backpack and headed up a ridge that was covered in short evergreen trees. Ken and Sabre followed.

Ken tried following Brodie's motions, carefully placing each step, amazed that a man of such size could walk so nimbly on a rocky terrain with jandals. Small rocks slid down in the wake of their steps. They traversed several ridges for a minute and came to a ledge that looked out upon a vast rocky terrain like a scar running down the length of the mountain.

To the right they could see far up to the snowy top, still a kilometer off. The smoke plume continued to billow out of the crater. A few of what must be news and observation helicopters and a small airplane appeared even higher up, like gnats around smoking embers. To the left, the terrain gave way to a ridge that appeared to snake down the length of the mountain. Rockslides pocketed the region, producing bare patches where the trees and shrubs had slid down into the ravine leaving behind raw patches of rock and earth.

Brodie put his binoculars to his eyes and slowly scanned the terrain for several minutes. Sabre stuck his nose in the air, sniffing left and right.

Ken saw nothing that would indicate human life had any presence in this harsh landscape. In the bottom of the ravine he could see signs of past water flow that had come down the mountain. The place was barren and raw. He saw how easy it was for the rocks and whole sections to slide away and tumble down, burying things in its path. He didn't want to think about the possibility of Maya's body being down there underneath a pile of rock.

"She's not here, Mate," Brodie said with confidence, lowering his binoculars.

"How can you be sure?" Ken asked.

"These rockslides are all old. Nothing in recent months. You can tell by the color of the exposed rock, see." He pointed one out and explained the shades of color that told him when the sides had fallen away.

"There's plenty places to get to. We could do this for a couple days and not reach all of them. This mountain is huge Mate. There's dozens of ski runs up there too with countless places for someone to get lost. As you come down the mountain there are more and more places where someone could fall into a ravine or a waterfall or down a ridge.

Ken felt a sinking feeling of hopelessness. Brodie tried to give a comforting smile. "But let's not lose hope; we'll find your friend." He placed a comforting hand on Ken's shoulder and gave it a little shake. Ken nodded, and they retraced their steps back to the Land Rover.

Over the next two hours Brodie took him to several more lookout spots and they repeated the same pattern of climbing through scrub bush and over boulders and scanning the terrain. Several times Ken shouted Maya's name and listened to his echo come back to him, followed only by the sound of the wind in his ears.

Going back down the mountain, they stopped and checked some of the few short stay huts that provided bunks and minimal facilities for backpackers and climbers. They were deserted with no sign of recent occupancy. They used the restroom and continued on.

At a turn off surrounded by ferns and bush that promised a ten-minute walk to a waterfall, they sat in the Land Rover and snacked on crisps and protein bars as Brodie pondered their next move. He looked over a map of the terrain on his iPhone, swiping this way and that, cocking his head from side to side. Sabre rested in the backseat, enjoying the drive and trips outside but oblivious to the nervous tension in the air.

Ken's phone pinged, and a notification appeared. He looked down at it. "What the...hell?" he whispered.

"What's up?" Brodie asked.

Ken shared the screen with him.

Maya's Nikon would like to share photos. Accept?

CHAPTER SIXTEEN

Ken spun his head left and right and checked the mirrors. The area was deserted. He hit accept, and they waited. They watched the ubiquitous digital wheel spin hypnotically as the device attempted to comply. Thirty seconds later a notification appeared, *Unable to Complete Request.*

"Her camera must be near here," Ken exclaimed, and they got out of the vehicle. He held his phone up, walking away from the vehicle and across the road. He looked out across the terrain in hopes of seeing something while watching his phone. Nothing changed. He ran back and began walking up the trail. He stopped, looking at his phone hopefully. After a minute nothing changed.

They walked back to the vehicle and got back in, sitting there watching his phone and wondering what it meant.

Maya's Nikon would like to share photos. Accept? popped up again.

"What the hell?" Ken pondered aloud again. He hit accept again, and they waited. "She shared some photos with me two nights ago. Unless my phone is going haywire to torment me, it's got to be somewhere." Again the phone reported it was unable to complete the request.

"Here, give me the phone," Brodie commanded, and Ken handed it to him. He stepped out of the vehicle and walked up a short berm and into the brush. Ken followed him to the top and looked in. Brodie was navigating a seemingly impenetrable decline through ferns and thickets like a bull wading through a marsh. He stopped twenty meters down the incline, holding the phone out before him, walking to one side and then the other. Ken could only faintly see him through the foliage. Brodie paused in silence for many seconds and then yelled, "It's coming through!"

Ken yelled out "Maya?!" into the forest and waited several seconds, his eyes scanning the foliage for any sign of her. There was only silence. He was tempted to go in after Brodie and see what the phone was doing, but resisted. There was a minute of silence, and then Brodie's voice came out of the wilds, "Oh hell, mate. Oh hell. This isn't good."

He came crashing back up through the brush, knocking over ferns and through thickets with his thick legs, clambering up the incline. He handed the phone to Ken who looked down at the image that had been received. A gasp came to his lips.

CHAPTER SEVENTEEN

The gears of the truck ground as Ruth moved it from first to second gear, nervously trying to navigate the pedals at her feet. She swore, regretting switching vehicles and letting them take the Land Rover with its various comfort buttons and automatic gears. Brodie's truck was an old gas-guzzling Ford F-150 filled with his own tailored gadgets and various cables for electronics. A semi-nude Polynesian dancer hung from the rearview mirror, and the car had a distinctive male smell only appreciated in certain scenarios she did not want to think about. She reminded herself she was only going a few blocks and could put up with it.

She pulled into the local police station on Clyde Street and walked in through the glass door, an electronic chime ringing through the small office building. Jasmine Wills, a young employee at the station working in casual dress, came through to the small reception to greet her. "Hi Ruth," Jasmine said, recognizing a familiar face.

"Hi Jas. How's your mom?" Ruth replied.

"Oh, she's still down in Wanganui, getting her treatments. She'll come back in two weeks to visit. Doctors are still positive we'll beat it." She sounded like she'd had to repeat that rehearsed response a hundred times. The news of her mother's cancer battle was well known around town, given how it disrupted the production of the best bakery for a hundred kilometers.

"That's good to hear," Ruth's answered. Her tone then went serious. "Look Jas; I just returned from having driven up past Taupo when I heard that the American photojournalist I personally know went missing, and so I came back to see what I could do to help."

"Oh yes, we received a missing person report on that," Jasmine replied with an artificial frown. "I put it on the website and sent alerts out to the officers in the field and the Park Rangers. I'm sure she'll be found or show up."

Annoyance showed on Ruth's face. "I got to know this women and am very, very concerned. She has not been seen in almost twenty-four hours and likely spent the night on that mountain. Is that all you can do? Is there anyone else here on duty?" she asked, irritated.

Jasmine flinched and became nervous. "Um, well, the mountain eruption has caused a little distraction to be honest. I'm the only one in the office, and even I'm here on an off day. I volunteered to come in because of the eruption. Our two helicopters are occupied with that too. But I'm sure once that is under control, we'll get a search party out looking for her."

There was a long pause as neither knew further how to respond. "Sorry," Jasmine said with a weak shrug.

Ruth went back out the front door, frustrated. She looked up at the mountain, spotting the tiny helicopters hovering at a distance from the smoke plume. She'd seen the mountain do this a few times in her life, and each time she felt the nervous excitement everyone else felt. Now she was annoyed by it, feeling it was taking resources away from finding a lost friend.

She drove down the street to the Mountain Rocks Cafe and Bar and parked outside. She ordered a pastry and latte and sat at a table outside where she could keep one eye on what Ruapehu was doing. The street was busy with the traffic of people coming down from the mountain and those who had decided to move out of town until the alert level came back down. She knew most of them left for economic reasons, knowing where there was no skiing there would be few customers in the hotels, restaurants, and shops. They were nearing the end of the ski season anyway, and this event might just preempt the annual economic slowdown.

Her coffee arrived and as she took her first sip, her phone pinged with a message from Ken. They'd been exchanging "nothing new" updates every hour or so. She opened the message and read it, her eyes going wide.

Found signal halfway up mtn. Maya's camera mysteriously sent me this image: Below the text was a clear shot of the Russian, Mr. Kiselevich, standing under the canopy of the forest, deep amongst ferns, a surprised frown on his face as he looked into the camera. He was wearing a camouflage hood. In his hand was a small cage containing the unmistakable shape of a kiwi bird. *Hunting for source of the image now*, came the next text.

Ruth's hands shook. She put two and two together, realizing if this was the last image Maya took with her camera, she was very much in harm's way, if not already past that point. Ruth tried to lift the small coffee cup to her lips again and found she couldn't do it without spilling it and so put it back down. She pulled a ten dollar note out of her purse and tossed it onto the table. She rushed back to the truck and with a grinding of the gears, raced back up the street to the police station.

"Jasmine!" she yelled into the empty reception.

She heard running footsteps, and Jasmine came through the door. "What is it?"

"Look at this!" Ruth exclaimed, holding her phone up for her to see.

Jasmine leaned forward, took in the image with a frown and cocked her head. "I don't get it."

Ruth was speaking quickly, "This is the man I evicted from a rental property yesterday. He and two other Russian men were renting a chateau on Mangawhero Terrace by the river. We received several complaints about them, and when they refused to let me inspect the property I ordered them out. My dog was barking at their van yesterday when I went over there. A lot of suspicious stuff was going on, and I was planning to report them to you. Look! They are capturing kiwis! They are poachers."

"Um, that's pretty bad, I agree." Jasmine took a moment to collect her thoughts, twisting her hands. "Um, there's a volcano going off out there, and I don't think this will make a whole lot of interest right now, so to speak. I mean if you want to fill out a report I can get it over to the Ministry of Agriculture and Forestry, and I'm sure they will want to look into it."

"You don't get it!" Ruth snapped at her. "This is the last photo taken by Maya's camera. This man caught her taking this photo of him in the act of his crime, and now she's missing. She has not been heard from or seen in a day!" Her tone turned to rage, the words coming out like bullets. "You have a *missing person*, likely *killed* by a Russian poacher on *your mountain*! An American of all people that works for National Geographic! This is happening on *your watch* while you are in here taking phone calls about missing cats. That mountain's going to do whatever that mountain is going to do," she said pointing to the sky. "We've seen this act before. This however," she said pointing at her phone, "we have not seen before." She leaned in close across the desk, her tone simmering. "I'm coming in here, and we're getting something going on this right now. You got that?"

Jasmine nodded and swallowed several times, tears building in her eyes. "Okay, okay."

"I'll be back in five minutes with the identification papers and data I have on these Russians, including their license plate and vehicle description. We are going to get it out to your officers, highway patrol and call in additional support to get a search going. Agreed?"

Jasmine nodded several times again.

CHAPTER EIGHTEEN

Ken finished sending the text to Ruth and looked up at Brodie. Each seemed to be asking the other what to do next.

"Maya's camera might be somewhere near and maybe her along with it," Brodie surmised. "We should start looking."

The idea of an unresponsive Maya lying injured or dead nearby made Ken sick to his stomach. He fought down a feeling of helpless panic and tried to focus his mind on what to do. He stepped over to the brush and peered inside. It was a jungle of thickets, trees, vines, and ferns all competing for space. They could search for hours and hardly have covered the visible terrain.

Ken tried calling Maya's cell phone a couple of times and listening to see if he could hear a ring or vibration somewhere. He walked along the berm and down the trail, looking and listening, and got nothing. He called her name into the brush several times, and there was no response. He was frustrated and tormented about what this photo and her absence meant.

An idea struck him, and he ran back to the Land Rover. He opened the side door and grabbed Sabre's leash, putting it back on the dog. He let the dog out of the vehicle and handed the leash to Brodie. He then went around to the back of the vehicle, pulling up the rear hatch. He opened a side pocket of his suitcase and pulled out the National Geographic camera strap Maya had given him. He held it by its ends, letting it dangle in front of him. "This was Maya's," he said to Brodie, who picked up on his plan, nodding. Ken knelt down before the dog, trying to look deep into its eyes, trying to make a strong connection. The dog licked his face and he grimaced. He brought the camera strap between them and Sabre instinctively began to sniff it eagerly, its tail wagging slightly "Maya," he said firmly. "Maya! *Where is Maya?*" he commanded and pointed towards the brush.

The dog took off, pulling Brodie along. The dog circled the parking area a couple times and then, nose down, began going along the path, away from the known location where the phone had received the photo. Ken and Brodie followed the animal as it went from one side of the path to the other, its nose furiously testing the ground and the air. They both looked at each other puzzled, and shrugged, letting the animal take them wherever it was going to.

A hundred yards along the path with trees and ferns canopying all around them, the dog suddenly veered off the path into the brush, crashing through shrubs and ferns. Brodie hopped along after Sabre, nimbly avoiding large branches and occasionally freeing up the leash when it got caught. Deeper into the brush they went until they came across another rarely used path. The dog followed the path quickly, and they stayed with it, regularly beating back fronds or branches that had grown into it. The dog pulled them into a clearing where it was evident some human activity had occurred. Branches and ferns were crushed down, and some food wrappers lay about. The dog sniffed in circles, going around the site several times, inspecting, and then ignoring each wrapper. After a few moments, when Ken thought the search had reached a dead end, it pulled them into the brush again. They went up an incline this time, climbing over roots and slippery rocks, their feet slipping on the undergrowth. Brodie had taken his jandals off by then and was panting and heaving as he tried to keep pace with the animal.

The dog stopped suddenly, its head buried in a bush, and let out a quiet yelp. It backed out of the bush, holding between its jaws a strap with a large Nikon camera dangling beneath.

"I'll be bloody damned!" Brodie said, resting his hands on his knees to catch his breath.

Ken went to his knees to take the camera from the dog, not believing his eyes. "Good doggie!" he said almost as an afterthought, taking the camera from its mouth. "Excellent doggie!" He said more eagerly, realizing that in fact he was holding Maya's Nikon. He looked the camera over. It appeared clean and unharmed. It was still on with the battery light blinking low. He flipped to image mode and saw the very photo it had sent him. He scanned back through them, Brodie looking over his shoulder. The shots showed the clearing they had just come from with two of the Russians in camouflage, one of them bent over with some equipment and cages at his feet. She had taken multiple images of them at work, some holding the birds up at eye level, one poking something like a stick into a cage. "The third guy must have surprised her," Ken murmured. The earlier shots showed her approach to the site, and from it they deducing the direction she had come from.

Sabre, not getting any more attention, whined and sat down on his haunches. He let out a little bark.

"He's demanding a treat for his find," said Ken. "We should have brought something."

Brodie reached into a pocket in his hoodie and pulled out a beef jerky stick wrapped in plastic. "This do?"

"Perfect," Ken replied.

He tore the jerky open, making Sabre's tail smash back and forth at the foliage. He tore it in half and dropped the piece from high, and the dog eagerly caught it. "That's for now," Brodie told the dog. "You get the other half if you find the body."

"Let's hope it doesn't come to that," Ken added quietly.

"Yeah, sorry Mate," Brodie apologized.

Using the camera's images as best they could, they began to trace back from the clearing to where she might have come. Thankfully she took multiple photos, but they found it hard to match them to any particular scene with so much similar looking foliage.

After a few minutes, the dog started pulling at the leash again, taking them down a faint path. "He wants the rest of that jerky!" Brodie said.

Moments later, they found her camera bag. It was propped up against a mossy boulder along with a water bottle. Her phone was in the bag side pocket, low on battery, but still alive. There were dozens of unseen text messages and voice mails.

Ken took photos of the site and what they found. He sent a report to Ruth with images. She responded she was at the police station now and demanding action.

They looked around the place for further signs of Maya and found nothing. They continued to call her name and got no response. The forest was undisturbed and empty, like these items had been mysteriously abandoned. Sabre was panting, needing a rest. They sat down on the undergrowth, each in their own thoughts. Birds called in the trees as sunlight filtered through the canopy. Insects made buzzing noises as they flitted about above them and occasionally landed on their face and ears. Ken heard the distinct call of the Tui bird as it descended onto a branch in the canopy above and wished he could have them tell him what happened here and where Maya was. The beauty of the forest was lost on him as he felt sick to his stomach with worry.

After ten minutes they got up, and Ken again put the camera strap before Sabre and earnestly asked the dog to find Maya. The dog seemed confused, sensing it had already accomplished this task. It wandered around the brush in circles and seemed to get into several distractions with animal holes and sounds only the dog heard. Then he appeared to have picked back up a scent, finding a trail and leading them along it. They wound through ferns and scrub for several more minutes, up inclines and then down, letting the animal lead them wherever its nose was pulling it.

Around a bend, they came upon a sight that at first puzzled them by the scene's incongruity with their surroundings. But there was no mistaking what it was.

"That was their rental," Ken said, despair in his voice.

CHAPTER NINETEEN

Ken yelled into the open air at the top of his lungs, "Maya!" and waited. A few birds took flight and then quiet returned. Only the rustle of leaves and gurgle of running water could be heard.

They carefully looked all around. Nothing else unusual was visible.

The car was front down in a shallow creek at the bottom of a thirty-meter steep slope. The trail of brush along the slope behind the car was torn up with wheel tracks that went clear to the top of the ridge. Ken realized the wandering path of their search had done a full oval, and they had come back probably several hundred meters down the mountain from the scenic waterfall turn-off they had stopped at.

They approached the car and saw that the front hood had buckled up from the impact, and the windshield had shattered. The driver's side was partly open and they could see no one in the front seats.

"Bro, this is a crime scene," Brodie commented, holding back Sabre who was eagerly tugging on the leash.

"If Maya is in that thing or nearby, I need to know right now, with or without the police," Ken answered.

"Right then," Brodie said as he nodded nervously. He pulled out his phone and began recording the scene, taking footage as they approached.

Ken called out for Maya once more, and again there was silence. He clambered through the brush and stepped into the creek, approaching from the side of the vehicle. He stepped on moss-covered rocks, water sweeping below his ankles. He looked into the passenger sideview windows, fearing what he might see. The seats were all empty. Recording as he went, he reached into the open driver's side door and released the boot. He noticed the rental key fobs were sitting on the dashboard, further confirming it had been intentionally pushed down the incline. The boot opened with a click and flipped back.

Brodie clambered up the slope and looked inside, his camera held out before him. "Travel bags and cases. That's all," he called back down.

"She's not here, and if she was, Sabre would have smelled her," Ken said. "I guess that's a relief." But then where was she? He assumed the men she had photographed had caught her, and finding them would lead him to her.

He called Ruth, and she picked up on the first ring and began immediately talking.

"Hey, I'm at the police station, working with the only lady here. I've given her all the information on the Russians that I have and she's put out another bulletin. I've scared her half to death, but she isn't much help. Probably good that I've donated to every fundraiser they've put on and buy her mum's..."

"We've found their car," Ken interjected, cutting her off. "No sign of Maya, but this is definitely a crime scene. The car was driven over the edge and smashed at the bottom of a creek. It's empty except for her luggage."

"Oh my gawd!" came Ruth's response, her worst fears being realized. "Oh my gawd."

"I'm sending you images and videos we've taken of the place."

"Send them to me, and I'll bring it back to them. I might have to go find some actual cops, because we're getting little attention here," she answered.

"The police aren't picking up on this yet?!" Ken asked incredulously.

"They are, but they are also consumed with handling matters related to the eruption and evacuation and ensuring everyone is out of danger," Ruth answered. "She's been missing for less than twenty-four hours, and their protocols..."

From the other side of the car Brodie raised his hands impatiently, "Are the police coming or what?" he asked.

Ken lowered the phone under his chin to tell Brodie what was happening. "Ruth's there at the station now, and reportedly there's only a lady who isn't too helpful," he replied with a shrug.

"Hmmph," Brodie snorted. "Jasmine. Typical. Alrighty then," he said defiantly. "We gotta make some noise to be heard, I guess."

Ken frowned as Brodie walked over to him and started going through apps on his phone. "No one can hear us from here, Brodie. We're halfway up a volcano."

"Ever heard of the Internet, Bro? I think you people there in Cali perfected it, right? Ever heard of that Facebook thing? It knows how to make noise. Tell Ruth I'm going to start live streaming from the Chateau Rentals Facebook page and to get herself over to wherever those media vans are and demand they pick it up. She'll know how to slap them around the ears and get them hopping. She's done it to me before."

"I heard him," Ruth said. "I'm on it." She hung up.

Ruth stepped back into the police station and looked over at Jasmine who gave her a puzzled *What is happening now?* look.

"You're being bypassed," Ruth told her. The two of them stood alone in the police station, tension in the air. Ruth pointed to the command station in the back with its rows of computer monitors. "Take me to the back," she commanded.

Jasmine did as she was told, the social hierarchy taking rank over office protocol. "Log your computer onto my Chateau Rentals website." Jasmine sat down, and Ruth directed Jasmine through to their Facebook page and saw that Brodie had indeed started a live stream from the car crash site.

She was shocked at the image. Brodie was narrating as he spoke into the camera being held by Ken, describing the scene behind him. He held up Maya's camera and her bag they'd found back on the trail. He pointed out the National

Geographic logo on her strap. He turned her camera around, and the image zoomed in on the photo of the Russian with the caged kiwi as Ken told the audience what they were looking at. Then he held up Ken's phone to the image of Maya taken days before on the Old Coach Trail. He told them this was the American photojournalist they were searching for. The video ended.

Jasmine put her hands to her mouth and started crying. Ruth hit her in the shoulder. "Link that video to your police website and send it to the various media websites. Send it to your commanding officer. Send it to Wellington. Send it to National Geographic, Send it to the US Embassy. Link it with that Volcano Cam. Blast it anywhere and everywhere. Let's go!"

Jasmine began nervously working the keyboard and mouse, her hands shaking, tears continuing to fall.

Ruth stepped aside and dialed Cynthia's number. After a few rings, she picked up with her voice audible through the roar of the helicopter engine. Ruth explained what they had found and said she was doing all she could to get the authorities involved. She described where the car had been found and said they should now be looking for a blue van the Russians were driving. Cynthia thanked her and said she was going to direct the helicopter to fly over to that region and see if they could help spot it.

Confirming the links had been sent by Jasmine and instructing her to get more people involved, Ruth headed out of the police station. She sat in Brodie's truck for a moment, sending an email blast to the thousands of Chateau Rentals contacts and hundreds of the citizenship of

Ohakune she had in her address book, linking the live stream and pleading in the message line for help in locating the missing photojournalist. She watched her message fly into the cloud and felt a brief sense of satisfaction.

Half as a prayer, she whispered to herself, "We're making some noise now, Babe. We're gonna find you."

CHAPTER TWENTY

Maya felt the van floor shift beneath her body as someone entered and moved over to where she lay. The hood was yanked free from her head and she looked up in fear, her eyes adjusting to the light.

The Russian was kneeling down, looking her over, concern on his face. She had spent most of the past eighteen hours on the floor in the van, her hands and feet bound. She felt she had slept some during the night, but didn't think it was more than a couple hours. The sound and smell of the caged animals she shared the space with kept her awake. She could hear the sorrow and lament in the tone of their chirps, and she shared their misery with her own crying.

Just yesterday she had said goodbye to new friends she wished she could stay with and get to know more. She felt the loss of driving away from them, especially Ken, whom she vowed to stay in touch with in the hopes there might be a future for her there. His note held this promise, and she had been dreaming of ways to make it possible.

Returning to a list of photos she wanted to capture, she had parked her car and backpacked across several sections of mountain ridges, capturing photos of the geological formations, boulders, cliff faces, and riverbeds created by past volcanic activity. She'd planned one last walk into an area of dense vegetation to capture a low waterfall that a local had told her about that was not on maps. Following his description of a rarely used trail, she been moving along it when she heard deep voices in a foreign language.

She approached slowly, placing her bag beside a boulder back on the trail so she could move stealthily. From a distance she could see they were working with traps and equipment, dressed in camouflage. She'd figured in an instant the only reason forest workers would wear camouflage would be to do something nefarious. She stayed back, hidden from sight, and zoomed in with her camera, taking photos of them. She could hear them talking gleefully amongst themselves and shook her head in disgust when she saw one hold a little cage up to his face and begin to poke into it with a stick, the bird thrashing around and chirping loudly. The man laughed and tossed the cage down.

After ten minutes of watching and capturing the scene, she slowly rose to back out and retrace her steps to her bag and call the authorities, when off to her left a man appeared out of the brush. He was holding a cage and looked as surprised to see her as she was to see him. She had the presence of mind to take a shot of him without raising the camera to her eye.

The man's face went from surprise to anger, and it crashed down on her the trouble she had now found herself in. He tossed the cage aside and leaped forward in the brush towards her. She took off running, adrenaline rushing into her blood. The man was shouting back to his comrades in Russian as he chased after her. She heard them shouting in return, joining the chase.

She was in full panic, running through dense thickets and foliage, trying to stay on a trail, but finding it impossible to locate. She cursed having left her phone with her bag. The leaves and branches scraped at her face and arms. She stole a look back and saw the man was thirty meters behind her. With his long legs and taller frame he was able to leap over and through the vegetation, easily keeping pace with her. She saw she was not going to outrun him. She pulled her camera from her neck as she ran and made a feeble attempt to hit the buttons that would send the photos to her phone. She couldn't slow down and was unable to control her finger motions. She pressed wildly at the camera, and turning a corner around some rocks, she tossed it wildly into the brush to her left.

Her arms now free to aid her balance, she kept going, panic increasing, her lungs burning as they strained for more oxygen in the higher elevation. She slid down a long incline on her backside and began to climb the ridge on the other side, grabbing at roots and plants to pull herself up. She attempted another quick look back, only to feel the full weight of the man's body slam into her, driving her to the ground.

She screamed, squirmed, and fought to get away, but was no match for his burly arms which pinned her hands to the ground. She continued to struggle until he hit had across the face with the back of his hand, the sharp pain stunning her into submission. A moment later, his friends joined him, all of them talking wildly in Russian. The larger one that had caught her began issuing orders to the others.

A few minutes later, her screams were cut off by a gag tied around her mouth. Her arms and legs were bound, and she was being carried back to their worksite. She was placed on the ground as they quickly packed up their gear, furtively keeping an eye on their surroundings for other observers. They carried her back to their van and placed her in the back with the birds they had collected. The last thing she saw was the Russian telling her, "It is okay, don't worry. It is okay," and then placing a bag over her head. They drove a short distance and stopped. She knew nothing of the language, but could tell there was arguing and strain in their voices as they talked over each other.

Ten minutes later she felt hands on her buttocks and hips, and a shudder of panic ran through her as she tried to scream. The hand felt over her pants and then forced themselves into her pockets. She felt vomit rising in her throat. Something was pulled from her pocket and the person left her. A moment later she head the familiar *beep-beep* of a car being unlocked, and then the sound of her rental being started and revved. A moment later there was a rush of bodies getting back into the van, the sound of latex gloves being removed, and then they drove away.

She tried the strength of the bonds. They were done with nylon rope. She could never break them and had little hope of finding a way to cut herself free. For some hours, they had ignored her, driving to two other locations, and bringing more cages into the van. She knew nothing of their language but could tell from their tone there were more arguments between them and crude jokes. She said nothing, wanting to disappear and hope they would forget about her.

Some hours later, her mouth dry and bladder bursting, she was picked up and taken out of the van. The cold air and insect racket outside the van told her it was night. Two of the men carried her into the brush, her backside scraping over ferns and shrubs. She began to sob, thinking they were going to kill her and hide her body. She attempted to scream and found she could only moan.

They placed her on the ground, and then the Russian said, "We help you stand," and she felt herself being picked up from behind her shoulders. The bag was removed from her head and she tried to look around, seeing only darkness in all directions. A camp light turned on and she saw she was standing in a forest, two of the Russians beside her, looking concerned. "Don't worry. You need water and toilet, yes?" asked the leader. She numbly nodded at him. "Okay, we take this away and you drink," and he reached behind her head, undoing the vice clamp that held the rag around her head. She felt her mouth come free and took in a deep breath. "No need scream, okay? No one for many, many kilometers. No one hear you." He said this like it was her choice to scream or not and he did not care. She nodded. He undid the bonds on her hands and placed a water bottle in them, which she drank from eagerly.

"We are good people, you will see. We don't want harm, but you could cause trouble, so we have you come with us. You will see at end we the good people." He tossed a roll of toilet paper at her feet and said, "You do business. Constantine will stand over there. If you try to undo legs, he stop you." He leaned in and quietly said, "He plead with me to find how you taste between the legs, so give him no reason to find this out, okay?" She nodded, and he stepped away.

Maya looked over at the lecherous man who was staring at her from ten feet away. She reached down and moved the light a few feet further away from her and then hopped behind a shrub so he could only see her back and slid down into the brush, unfastening her pants. Her job done, she allowed him to come over and rebound her hands. The other Russian returned, and she was carried back to the van which appeared to be parked in the middle of the forest.

They left the gag off her head, but put the hood back on. She was placed on the floor behind the passenger seats again, and a blanket was placed over her. She could hear two of them had taken the front seats, putting the chairs back. She assumed one of them took turns outside on watch while the guys in the van slept. She cried off and on during the night, kept awake by their snoring and the sounds of the rustling, scratching, and chirping of the caged birds.

And now here she was, her captor squatting before her with daylight coming in from the front of the van.

He reached out and slowly brushed aside the locks that had fallen on her face. She flinched back, banging her head on the side of the van. "You are pretty, you know?" he shrugged. "You can scream, as I tell you. No problem. No one hears."

Maya stared back at him, doing all she could to mask the fear she felt. "Water," she whispered.

"Yes, course. You need water to live." He unscrewed the lid from a plastic bottle and carefully placed it between her bound hands so she could bring it to her lips. He watched her take sips from the bottle, nodding appreciatively. "Hungry?" he asked. Maya hadn't eaten in twenty-four hours but felt anything she tried to eat would come right back up. She shook her head.

The man shrugged, sitting down on the van floor across from her. He pulled a handgun from his backside and held it across his knees as he propped his shoulders against the side of the van.

"You see... Ma...ya," he said, holding up and carefully reading her photojournalist identification card that she had kept in her pocket but he must have removed when he took her car keys. He read her name, turning it over in his hand. "We just like you Americans. We seek profit for our benefit." She watched as he took his phone out and took a photo of her ID card, front, and back. "I do this here so we open with each other, and you know from me I am man of my word, as you say. You agree to return to normal life after we gone and say nothing and we leave you alone. You don't agree, and we then find you wherever you are and then magic," he made a throat-slitting motion with his fingers, "you no longer stop in our... what you call it?... enterprise," he said with a remembering nod.

Maya nodded her head, her mind resisting the discussion.

"You know why you still alive?"

Maya didn't know how to answer that question.

"Let's go," he instructed and got back up on his haunches, untying her legs. "You walk with us, I explain. But your hands stay like this. No stupid business and no trouble for Maya."

They got out of the van, and she was led between them, into the brush, glad to get her legs moving and able to breath normally without a gag in her mouth. She was in fact hungry, but had little appetite.

CHAPTER TWENTY-ONE

B rodie gave Sabre the other half of the jerky stick to the dog's delight. They carefully made the climb up to the top of the ridge from where the car had plunged, pulling on vines and thin trees to get to the top. There they saw the turn-off where Maya must have parked and the break in the brush where the car had been directed along its path to plunge down to the creek. Continuing to video the scene from above, Brodie described what he was seeing and what must have happened to the car.

Traffic on the website was multiplying by the millisecond as people around Ohakune and around New Zealand, and even some around the world picked up on the story.

"I need my bag, Bro. We need to GoPro this," Brodie said with a determined look.

They headed up the steep road to where they had parked the Land Rover.

As Ken was changing into dry shoes a text came in from Ruth telling them the link was being streamed everywhere she could think of and that they should now be looking for the blue van the Russians were driving. She said she'd told Cynthia in the helicopter, who was now directing her pilot over to their area to help in the search.

Opening his backpack, Brodie got out a bowie knife which he slipped into the back of the waistband of his shorts. He tossed a flashlight to Ken and put a backup battery pack into his pockets. He then placed a GoPro camera on a headband to his forehead. He turned to Ken, "I'm ready Bro."

They took a look up the mountain to witness a second small blast of ash and smoke pour forth, giving it now two plumes of smoke. It shot up what could have been several hundred meters into the air with black rocks and sediment particles raining back down on the crater while white smoke billowed forth. They heard the latent blast as a distant boom and watched as the plume of ash continued to climb into the sky.

"She's not happy," Brodie said with a shake of his head. His phone chimed, and he looked down. "Yeah, they've raised her to a level *Three* now. Telling everyone to stay away from the rivers, valleys, and bridges. You know, all the stuff that a lahar could travel down and cause damage to." He looked up at Ken, reading the face of an anguished man who looked even more worried. "No worries, Mate! I'll look after ya. We got this."

They discussed what could have happened to the blue van. Ken's first assumption was they already left the area as they didn't see any van on the road up or down, but this was only one of three access roads to the top. By now, they could be halfway across the country. They knew from the time of the last photo Maya took with the camera and her phone that she went missing around 3:00 pm yesterday. That was twenty-two hours ago, and in that time anything could have happened. As they had a license number and description of the van, he assumed an alert going to all highway patrol in the country could also locate it at some point in the near future. He felt sure they would find them somehow, but he realized he didn't care about finding them. He wanted to find Maya. She was what mattered to him. He realized this as a little shock to himself when he saw the significance of finding her was more than just finding a friend. He was sure he was finding someone he had fallen in love with.

"Let's keep driving and looking around. It's the least we can do," said Ken, walking to the driver's side.

As he was about to get in, a helicopter roared overhead, and he looked up. It was almost close enough for him to see the people inside, and he thought he recognized Cynthia sitting beside the pilot, her face scanning the mountainside.

They pulled out of the turn-off and headed back down the mountain road.

CHAPTER TWENTY-TWO

"Hey guys! I've just been in the Channel 3 media van where your video is playing on the news, and the story is being picked up by the broadcast alongside the volcano updates. We've got a couple of police officers here with us, and a search party is being assembled now to head up the mountain," Ruth's voice reverberated through the vehicle on speaker.

Sabre barked at the sound of her voice. "Good dog, Sabre!" she yelled. He barked again.

"How did you get in the media van?" Ken asked in astonishment.

"Um, I opened the door and walked in. This is New Zealand. No one locks their door. And the news is always looking for a breaking story, and we've got one. But here's the deal," she added, "Cynthia thinks she's found their van."

Ken braked and pulled over to the side of the road. "Where? Where do we go?"

"Well look, the authorities here have told me to tell you to hold off on going there. They want to get a proper response team in place."

Ken shook his head, and he saw Brodie grit his teeth.

"Now that I've relayed that message, as I promised them I would, here is how you get there," and she proceeded to describe an unmarked entrance to a rangers-only dirt road that curled around to the south-western side of the mountain, five minutes from where they were. She said the van appeared to be hidden beneath some trees about a kilometer along the road, near its end."

"I know the road," Brodie said with certainty. "We're heading there now."

"Please be safe, boys. No Rambo stuff, okay? You've seen these guys Ken; they're not ones to mess with. If you just locate and keep them in your sights, that's best. The authorities could be there in an hour or so."

"Ten-four, we got that," said Ken.

Five minutes later Brodie instructed Ken to slow down and then had him pull off on a thin dirt road to the right that would have been missed by any casual driver. He had to slow down considerably as the road was barely wide enough for their vehicle and on the left, fell away to steep mountainsides with ferns and tufts of grass clinging to the edge. Branches and leaves slapped against the driver's side on the right as Ken maneuvered to keep clear of the edge. The vehicle bobbed up and down as they traversed over rocks, puddles, and pits in the road. Brodie rolled down his window and stuck his head out to try to see clearer around bends.

They continued like this for a few minutes until Brodie motioned for them to stop. "It's going to be right up there. The road ends not far ahead."

Brodie checked the GoPro camera on his head and ensured through his phone it was feeding live to the website. He opened his door and looked out. His next step would be a drop going steeply down a couple of hundred meters. "I think I'm getting out on your side," he said modestly to Ken. He attempted to slide his bulk into the backseat of the vehicle so he could exit the right-side passenger door and promptly got stuck. Sabre began to lick his face and the camera from the backseat as Brodie twisted and heaved, taking several attempts to un-wedge himself, repeatedly cursing Sabre. He finally got outside the door with Sabre on the leash.

They walked quickly, following the road around several turns, and spotted the van ahead, parked in a canopy of trees and bushes, as Cynthia had described. The ground had leveled out, and the vehicle had been driven up over a berm and into the foliage, partly concealed by thickets of shrubs and ferns. They waited back on the edge of the road for several minutes until they were sure no one was around. Cautiously approaching with Sabre sniffing the air, they reached the van and walked around it, pushing through the undergrowth. It was the van as Ken remembered it. The sides were windowless, and the small rear door windows had been covered from the inside. The front seats were empty except for some water bottles and bags beside the seats.

Sabre began wagging his tail excitedly, pulling in the direction further down the road and sniffing the ground repeatedly. "He's picked up a scent again. I hope it's Maya," Ken said. "They might have her with them." He felt a sense of hope she was alive.

"I want to know what's going on with this van," Brodie said and pulled the knife from his backside. He knocked on the rear door and stepped to the side, his arm ready to swing at any threat. "Anyone in there?" he asked loudly. Again there was only silence.

With a fast stabbing movement, he brought the hilt down on the rear window, shattering it. He waited a moment and, hearing nothing, reached his hand into the window, pushing aside the fabric covering that had been taped over it, and unlocked the door. He pulled it open, and they looked inside.

His GoPro video stream sent a live feed into the police station, media van, and several other thousands of devices, all revealing the same thing. Stacked in the back of the van were around two dozen small cages, each containing a live kiwi bird. The animals reacted to the light intrusion, chirping and turning rapidly in their enclosures. Behind the cages further empty cages, equipment cases, ropes, and tools were strewn about.

"I'll be bloody damned," Brodie said after a moment of stunned silence.

Sabre began to excitedly whimper, crouch, and shake his backside, confused and eager to be given a command to do something. "Hush Sabre," Ken commanded, and the dog toned it down a notch. Ken shook his head as he looked over the van contents, taking some photos with his phone and sending them to Ruth.

Ruth called him, speaking in a solemn voice. "We're seeing this," she said. "Oh, we're seeing it all right. And so is New Zealand. This is going to set some people's hair on fire."

CHAPTER TWENTY-THREE

Ken completed the call with Ruth and turned to Brodie. "You want to stay here and set these little fellas free while I go back with Sabre and bring the Land Rover forward so the police can reach here?" he suggested.

"Definitely," Brodie replied, hatred in his eyes.

Ken realized his words were to an audience of more than one. "On second thought, this is also a crime scene. Shouldn't we turn these birds over to authorities to properly investigate and release them into the wild?" he asked calmly.

Brodie shook his head assuredly, his face in a grimace. "Do you not see the mountain up there? It is no coincidence these animals are being poached on the land of this mountain, and the mountain, she is angry. Oh yes, I've been saying it. She's angry. And so am I. We release these back to the mountain now or there may be a price none of us wishes to pay."

Ken paused in his thinking, looking at Brodie, seeing a side of him that came from deep in the man's culture and upbringing that he had not seen before. There was no superstition or faith in this man's mind. It was primal and fundamental knowledge that had been bred in his genes for centuries.

He pointed up to the GoPro, "That thing still on?"

"Yeah Mate, it's on, and it's not turning off," Brodie replied, steel in his voice.

"Good," Ken replied with a nod. "See you in a few minutes," and he headed back down the road at a jog, pulling Sabre along with him.

When he returned with the Land Rover several minutes later he saw the back of the van was wide-open, and the cages gone. He parked and got out with Sabre on his leash.

Brodie was deep in the brush, his back to him and on his knees, unmoving. The cages were scattered around him. As Ken approached, the big man didn't move. The cages were all open and empty. There was no sign of the birds. Brodie was speaking softly in Maori, his eyes closed. Ken came up beside him and squatted down, not wanting to disturb him in what could only be a prayer. He waited until Brodie finished speaking in an unrecognizable language and opened his eyes, and looked over.

"You did it."

"Yeah," Brodie said with a firm nod. "Now let's go find those bastards."

Ken was thinking of talking him out of it and was going to suggest again waiting for the police to arrive. He looked into the Maori's eyes and saw there was no stopping him now. "Fine, but we're not going to get ourselves killed or do something vengeful, agreed?”

Brodie nodded and slowly got to his feet. “Yeah, I know, Bro.”

CHAPTER TWENTY-FOUR

"You alive because I not a murderer," The Russian said, touching his chest with some pride as he walked beside her. "I am only man of business."

Maya stared up at him, slowly nodding, wanting him to say whatever he had to say for the man's own ego. In his own twisted logic, what he was doing was right, and she had no desire to contradict him or engage in a debate that would upset him.

"What you see in van, Maya?" he asked, directing his thumb back in the direction they had come from.

"Kiwi birds?" Maya responded, knowing it couldn't have been the answer he was looking for.

They entered a thin trail, brushing ferns and branches aside. "Yes, the famous and hard-to-find kiwi. Do you know most people in New Zealand have never seen kiwi not in zoo? It is night bird, hiding all the time. If tomorrow all kiwi's disappeared, the New Zealand people that call themselves Kiwi—they would not know. Do you know this?"

Maya shook her head. "So?"

"The whole thing of kiwi as symbol of country—that idea stupid. These people say themselves is Kiwi but they don't see kiwi. No, not kiwi in our van. We see money. What you look at about two million dollars." He said it again slowly, "Two—million—dollars," tasting the number on his lips with a smile. "Why that two million? We not care. Why some crazy Asian pay this much for birds? We not care. Maybe they rare or have special thing, you know? Maybe something in eggs give men better sex or make women boobies stay up or give people long life. We not know. This two million could go to New Zealand country, but New Zealand country say 'no, kiwi not for sale.' Well, now country lose two million and we get two million. Very simple, eh? You call 'economics,' yes? This economics. I giving you lesson on economics."

Maya nodded, showing her understanding. "If it's just economics, why then do you have to hold a gun on me?" Maya asked quietly and wishing right away she had not asked.

He reached back and tapped the gun in his waistband, and nodded. "You are American, yes? In America, more guns than people. In the movies everyone has a gun. The good guys and bad guys. To protect themselves. I have a gun to protect myself. American thinking, yes?"

Maya could only nod.

"Today we pick up last traps, and we leave this place. The mountain smoking if you did not know. This good thing. We drive away from town tonight, and you come with us.”

Maya thought about being forced to go with these men and what Cynthia must be thinking with her missing. “I have a partner here. She will be looking for me. People will be looking for me. Can I let them know I am okay?” she asked.

“No. They worry, yes. But you find good reason to say you lost and how you got to where we take you. You make it okay.” He stopped and smiled at her, and she forced herself to return a smirk, nodding at him, hoping she had gained some trust that would keep her alive.

“I know you, Maya,” he added. “You do as I say because you want to live. You smart girl.”

They trekked down and up inclines, one of the Russians using a handheld device that pointed out the locations where the traps had been laid. After an hour, they had one more bird and six cages that had caught what Maya assumed were weasels or stoats. They were released back into the bush with annoyance and curses from the men.

They rested under the canopy of a beech and shared with Maya more water and a packet of pretzels, which she ate hungrily.

They stayed under the cover of the thickets and trees as they slowly moved along, avoiding areas like creek beds or rock outcroppings where the sun shined through. Several times the distant sound of helicopters high above reached them.

At one point a helicopter roared directly overhead causing one of the Russians to throw her to the ground, as he searched the sky through the foliage, trying to spot it. It disappeared and they got back up and resumed their trek.

A few times one of the Russians talked to their leader and gestured at her, seeming to disagree with something about her presence. Each time the conversation was short, the leader brushing off whatever concern or idea they had. She thought about past stories she'd heard of journalists being held as hostages, tortured, injured, and shot in the line of their work. She had always known there were dangers, but this country of only a few million people that is arguably one of the safest and kindest in the world—it was not somewhere she expected to find herself in the worst trouble of her young life.

CHAPTER TWENTY-FIVE

"This last stop," the Russian told Maya. "Then we leave."

The path had taken them to a section of the mountain's forest where the ground had leveled for a few acres and then ended with an edge that dropped down into a steep gorge. After being only under the shaded canopy of the trees, Maya wished she could be out in the open, visible or where they could be spotted and hopefully caught. Her captors were overly cautious she noticed. One of them seemed to be watching her at all times. She knew running was pointless, but also felt returning to their van and remaining a hostage while they drove away and traveled far from this place would only make her chances of escape harder. She didn't trust their promises to release her. She knew Cynthia would have the mountain being searched and would know how to pull in the right authorities to help, but most likely too late.

The Russians went along the edge of the foliage, hunting for the traps they had laid, while Maya was instructed to stand there. Her hands bound and nothing to do, she could only watch and listen to the sounds of the insects and trees rustling around them. One of them pulled up a cage, empty. He cursed and slung it over his back. They were having little success in this trip she saw and it was annoying them. Each empty cage meant less money for them and another kiwi still free.

A dog bark echoed from somewhere near.

All the men froze in their tracks, swiveling their heads to locate the source of the sound. Maya's heart started pounding heavy in her chest. The dog barked again, and Maya thought she recognized the sound and heard faint rustling of foliage in the distance. "Sabre?" she wondered aloud to herself.

The leader of the men stepped over to her. "You know dog?" he asked.

She shrugged. "It sounds like the dog of a family I met," she replied.

The man shook his head, frustrated with the hindrance to his plans. He pulled the gun from behind his belt and held it in the air. He motioned for his two comrades to start stepping backward towards the edge of the forest where no one could surprise them from behind and pulled Maya backward along with him.

"Hey! Who there?" he demanded, yelling into the foliage around them.

There was no answer. The Russians all looked around carefully and saw nothing move, continuing to step backward towards the edge of the trees.

"Who there?" he demanded again, angrily. "Someone there?"

Again there was only quiet.

He motioned the gun towards Maya's head. "Show yourself or I shoot girl," he demanded. Maya flinched away, shutting her eyes tight. "Show self now!"

A voice spoke out, "Okay, we will show ourselves."

Maya's body went numb with relief to hear Ken's voice and see the silhouettes of he and Brodie fifty meters off, deep in the brush. She had no idea how they'd found her, but she felt both relief and, then, fear for their safety.

"Come here!" the Russian demanded.

They began slowly walking through the brush, their hands at chest level.

"We have no gun," Ken said as they got closer. "We want no one to be hurt. We just want to bring Maya back with us." Sabre was now barking repeatedly, pulling hard on the leash.

The Russian shook his head and cursed in his language. "Another damn American," he exclaimed in English and cursed again.

They came within throwing distance of the men and stopped, Sabre continuing to bark and growl. The Russian stood there with the gun at his side, appearing annoyed. Ken could see Maya's hands were tied, and she looked disheveled and frightened.

"Shut up dog or I shoot it," the man said.

Ken pulled hard on Sabre's leash and commanded him to be quiet. Sabre stood still, growling quietly, his body quivering.

Brodie strangely seemed the calmest of them all. His hands had returned to his side, and he stood there, confronting the men with no sign of emotion. Ken looked over and tried to read what the big guy was thinking and got nothing.

"We would like our friend to come back with us," Ken said, hoping his voice carried some authority.

"No, sorry. She stay with us now. She do science project with us and stay with us," the Russian replied. "We do science and not understand why you interrupt," he added, appearing to think he could bluff himself out of his situation.

Ken felt his phone vibrate in his pocket. He thought it was likely Ruth trying to call him, seeing all this exchange happening live. He wanted to take the call, but knew doing so would be threatening to their survival, so ignored it.

Brodie spoke for the first time, his voice more sonorous than usual, a penetrating echo through the region, "Poaching kiwis from Aotearoa is not science. It is a crime."

"What the hell you know about crime?" the Russian retorted.

Brodie spoke again, his tone severe, "The birds you caught in your van have been set free. And any others you have will also be free. None will leave this mountain." He seemed to be speaking on behalf of the country, its people, and the mountain itself. Ken looked over at Brodie and was struck again by that strange sense of calmness over the man.

It took a moment for the Russian to realize what he had said and what it meant. Shock flashed across his face. The other Russians, seeing him fluster, fired questions at him in their language, trying to understand what was happening. He waved them away. He began to growl and turn red with rage, realizing that he had been hours away from seeing the success of weeks of work, and now it had been ruined. He raised the gun threateningly at Brodie.

"Stop! No!" Ken commanded, holding out his hands. "No shooting!"

Brodie continued to stand, defiant, unfazed by the gun now trained on him.

"Look at him!" Ken commanded, pointing at Brodie. "That is a camera on his head, streaming live. You are being recorded live right now. Think about it. You shoot, and your life is also over. Please, lower the gun," Ken pleaded with the man.

The Russian seemed to consider this, his rage turning to puzzlement as he understood the dilemma he faced. He slowly lowered the gun to his side, his bottom lip quivering with rage.

"Thank you," Ken said with a noticeable sigh.

The Russian slowly shoved the gun back in the rear of his waistband and placed his hands on his hips, his face remaining in a grimace.

Brodie's eyes never left the Russian. He slowly raised his hands to his chest and gripped his hoodie's collar along with the tank top underneath. He held them tight and began to methodically tear the fabric down the middle. His bulging forearm muscles flexing as the fabric separated like tearing paper. He took slow steps forward, pulling the garment down his back, freeing each arm, which he held out at his side, palms up.

"Brodie?" Ken asked in a worried whisper.

"What hell is this?" the Russian asked, looking at Maya and then the other Russians beside him.

Brodie came within twenty meters of the men, his face showing a fire of determination. His large muscular body, a landscape of artistic swirls and Koru designs, crawling over his pecs, shoulders, and abdomen.

Lowering to a squatting position, Brodies arms went akimbo to his thighs. His eyes bulged, and he let out a loud menacing snarl that reverberated through the forest. Everyone took an instinctive step back from him, including Ken.

Brodie's tongue shot out in a threatening grimace, and his eyes danced in a wild motion.

The Russians had never seen such a display before. Confusion and fear showed on their faces as they swore and began to rapidly ask questions none could answer. They wondered if the man was crazy, but felt a primal terror of him, like being faced with by a raging bear.

The leader came out of his shock and slowly pulled the gun back out and raised it, sighting it again on Brodie. He was responding not with anger as he had a moment earlier, but with terror.

It seemed at that moment everything went into slow motion as Hell rose up to claim the Earth.

CHAPTER TWENTY-SIX

A shuddering moan came from deep beneath the ground as the mountain all around them began to shake, the ground, trees, and branches trembling and quivering.

The glaring Maori with protruding tongue and eyes and the shaking ground were foreign and unknown experiences. The Russian's minds froze. The leader squinted one eye, futilely trying to still his trembling hand despite the tremor beneath him.

He squeezed the trigger. The shot was barely heard over the roar of the earth. He opened both eyes and saw he had missed. It was impossible to hold a steady aim.

Brodie, detached and exterior to his bodily self, sensed an untold power within and without. He began the motions of the Haka, his voice boomed over the noise of the terrain as he reached up and pulled the strength and might of his ancestral lines down into his body.

His arms and eyes reached up to the heavens as he performed the ritual he had learned and practiced all his life. A performance calling upon the power of deities and ancestors, created to intimidate, impress and humble one's enemies. He pulled his arms down and slapped his thighs and stamped his feet.

Across New Zealand thousands watched the event unfold live on their phones and home computers. They recognized the familiar Haka chant performed at ceremonies and sporting events and followed along in their minds. Some whispered from their porch seats and deck chairs, some made only gestures of the motions with their arms and legs that the ceremony called for, some raised themselves from their couches or stopped in their tracks and joined in the performance. But each of them, whether participating or not, felt their heart and soul pulled in the same direction as the call went out to claim and empower the heritage and honor of their land.

The Russian tried again to steady his aim, applying pressure to the trigger.

Maya twisted from where she was standing and leapt at the man with all the strength her legs could give her. She slammed into his open flank with her bound hands as the gun went off again, the shot sailing wide. They both fell to the ground. She scrambled to her knees, stumbling from the shaking ground, and tried to get up to run.

Ken saw Maya shove the man and go to the ground with him. He instinctively began to move toward her. The ground shook beneath his feet, but he managed to leap over the nearest shrub and began to tear through bushes toward her, stumbling and lurching with each step.

KA-BOOOOOMMMM!!

From the volcano's crater high above them a deafening explosion tore through the land as if several atom bombs detonated atop the mountain.

The shock wave ripped through the soul of all living things.

Time froze as senses and consciousness halted. Thinking, seeing, and hearing disappeared as though under a concussion.

In a mighty jolt the ground lifted upwards several inches and dropped down as effortless as a snapped bedsheet.

Everyone but the Maori collapsed to the earth. Bodies slowly writhed on the ground, for a moment lost for orientation and awareness.

Fastened hard in his stance, Brodie continued to chant and posture, his hands quivering, his eyes afire, and fury on his face.

ngā rua rerarera
ngā rua kuri kakanui i raro! Aha ha!

The foliage around them shook violently as the ground continued to undulate, sending clouds of dust and loose undergrowth billowing around the shade of the canopy, which shook as though under cyclone winds from all directions.

Still Brodie continued, his hands pounding on his chest and forearms, his feet stamping.

CHAPTER TWENTY-SEVEN

An hour earlier Cynthia and her pilot had risen to a height a kilometer from the crater, upwind from the plume and remained stationary. At this distance they were able to see the crater lake clearly and the plumes pouring from the edges. She felt safe to observe and document the event with a camera rolling and a laptop open to the sites showing her feedback from various seismic and volcanic instruments located around the mountain. She was not one of the scientists assigned to monitor the mountain, but could understand everything they were seeing and was thrilled to be permitted to have a first-hand view of the action.

Half of her mind however was back with the search for Maya. Ruth was giving her updates, and she knew they were close to locating her or finding out what had happened.

She was looking at her phone, and about to connect through to a link Ruth sent her when out of the corner of her eye the mountain seemed to come alive. She was unprepared for the sight of something so huge and stable seeming in a matter of seconds to fall apart and morph into a raging furnace of power.

A second earlier the crater lake had been a flat blue expanse with steam coming off, half-hidden by the plumes. It then seemed to quickly buckle, like a large plug had been pulled from underneath it. Then the crater disappeared behind a wall of pyroclastic rock and ash that exploded upwards, rising in just seconds to the height of their helicopter.

A moment later, she heard and felt the shockwave rip through the chopper like a bolt of electricity to her body. The blow pushed them back as if a gust of wind had hit a fly. The pilot struggled with the controls, his vision blurred and objects spinning.

"Pull away! Pull away!" she screamed.

Recovering some of his senses, the pilot pulled back on the joystick as they watched in stunned awe as thousands of tons of rock and ash blasted skyward, ripping into the heavens to heights far taller than the volcano itself. Edges of the volcano's crater fell away like flakes from a pastry as boulders the size of houses flew a kilometer skyward and came crashing down.

Like the ever-continuing explosion of a firework finale, the mountain spewed forth, sending ever more dark clouds of pyroclast billowing into the air. It came out at an alarming rate, generating bolts of lightning that cracked and slithered around the plume, like veins on a pulsating muscle.

Ruapehu had woken up.

CHAPTER TWENTY-EIGHT

The Russian rose to his knees, his sight a blur and ears ringing from the shockwave. The ground continued to shake and ripple beneath him, waves of force pulsating through it like ocean waves under a buoy. Lighting cracked through the sky, sending bursts of bright light through the canopy. He realized through the haze he had dropped the gun and reached for it, missing a couple of times and then fumbling with its grip.

Ka mate, ka mate! ka ora! ka ora!

Maya had made it only a few meters before she had collapsed. She was unable to right herself with all the shaking and the dizziness from the explosion. Her ears throbbed. Her body was finding it hard to move, and she couldn't see through the dust.

Ken forced his mind to concentrate and, unable to see, continued to crawl on all fours, pushing through shrubs and ferns, heading in the direction he'd seen Maya go down.

Brodie was a specter in a fog of dust, his strong voice unwavering, his intent strong and undiminished.

Ka mate! ka mate! ka ora! ka ora!
Tēnei te tangata pūhuruhuru

Ken reached Maya and grabbed her bound hands. She responded to his pulling, and she rose to her knees. He began to pull her back.

The Russian turned to the sound of the Maori, a voice joining with the roar of the volcano to torment and terrorize him. His eyes were wild with fear. He found the source of his suffering and concentrated all his might in aiming his sights on it. On his knees with one hand on the ground, he tried raising the gun once more.

Nāna nei i tiki mai whakawhiti te rā
Ā, upane! ka upane!
Ā, upane, ka upane, whiti te ra!

Then, beneath his body, the ground disappeared.

Ken, who was holding fast to Maya's bonds as he pulled her towards him, felt her suddenly drop away from him into bright daylight.

CHAPTER TWENTY-NINE

When the blast wave of the eruption hit the media van, it distorted everyone's senses, and audio feeds. Inside the vehicle, it sounded like someone had let off a grenade in the enclosed space. Ruth stumbled out along with the other occupants, her ears ringing, and looked up at the mountain. The ground beneath her feet trembled and pulsated, but she was able to stay upright.

She stepped a few paces away and watched in stunned awe as high atop the mountain gushes of rock blasted upwards from the crater. The ash plume continued to rise ever higher, a seemingly endless fountain that began to catch an air current high in the sky and spread outwards. It was already many kilometers up and continued to boil ever higher. Lightning snaked and crackled around the base of the plume.

She shook her head slowly in admiration and awe at the raw power. She whispered to herself, "That's right, Babe, let it out. Let it all out."

On the sidewalks around her, people had stepped out of the restaurants and stores and stood in their tracks, phones held skyward, slack-mouthed. Some were hustling away with their eyes repeatedly looking up at the volcano. She noticed cars were stopped on the roads, the passengers out on the asphalt, holding up their cell phones and talking excitedly.

The wail of backup emergency vehicles arriving to the town seemed to awaken people, and they began to get back into their cars or rush to where they were headed.

The volcano emergency evacuation sirens then started to wail around the town, rising and falling in pitch like an air-raid warning. The one-thousand town residents knew what that meant: Evacuate *immediately*. It would be only minutes before lahars and ash would come crashing down the mountain, with threats of tearing up the river paths, knocking over homes and power lines, swamping roads, and tearing away bridges.

Ruth could see this was the once-in-a-lifetime eruption that was going to top them all. Ruapehu had reached level *Five*, the highest possible.

She began to walk quickly back to Brodie's truck to join the others moving to get to safety. It was like walking atop a generator, the ground pulsating through her feet.

Her mind went back to the people close to her, trapped on the mountain. She looked back to her phone to see what was happening. When she saw the feed coming from Brodie's camera, she stopped and almost fell to her knees.

CHAPTER THIRTY

The edge of the gorge had collapsed in a landslide, taking the three Russians with it in a cascading descent of trees, foliage, rock, and dirt.

The ground had begun to calm, though tremors rippled like wavelets in a pond.

Where a second before Brodie had been standing in a canopy of shade and dust, daylight suddenly came to where he stood, just a few meters from the edge. He stepped forward and then leaned, looking down, witnessing the last of the sliding debris, fifty meters below. There was no sign of the men who, just moments before had been standing on secure ground.

He felt no sense of accomplishment or pride in what had happened. The Haka had been an instinctive response as if he was a vessel for the infinite. What had happened was a creation by Nature and from forces of far greater complexity and power than anyone could conceive.

He came out of his brief shock and looked over, seeing Ken was lying at the edge of the precipice, his head over the edge, shoulders, and arms straining. A blood-curdling scream came from over the side. Brodie stumbled over to Ken and lay down next to him, looking over the side. Ken had Maya by her bonds as she dangled in open space. Brodie reached down, grabbing the loose end of the rope. With the ease of lifting a full bucket, he helped pull Maya up and over the top. All three of them scrambled back into the brush. Sabre bounced between them, yelping and licking.

They sat there panting, coughing and collecting themselves for a moment, feeling the ground slowly calm to a mild thrum as the mountain continued to issue forth rock and ash.

Brodie pulled out his knife and cut the bonds holding Maya's hands. With her arms now apart, she pulled them both in for a hug, tears rolling. They knelt like that, heads interlocked, feeling the adrenaline leave their bodies in a heartfelt embrace. Having caught her breath, she repeatedly thanked them over and over between sobs. She told them she loved them and made promises to somehow repay them and will forever be in their debt. Brodie tried a couple times to modestly interrupt her with "Okay Lovey... yeah, yeah... all good..." and Ken attempted to acknowledge but it didn't stop or slow her down. She cried more, thanking, and praising them.

Ken pulled her up, looking into her eyes. He put a finger to her lips, and she stopped mid-sentence, frozen in her tumult of thoughts. They came together, lips naturally meeting, and embraced once more, this time in a rush of passion. For several moments nothing else mattered. Ken felt a natural bond form as two beings spiritually combined in an unbreakable embrace.

"Well, that shut her up," Brodie said with a chuckle, looking away.

Ken broke from Maya and looked over at Brodie with a big smile. He then frowned, asking, "That thing still streaming?"

Brodie fumbled with the phone in his pocket and looked up with a sheepish grin, "Yeah, sorry, Bro, still going. Probably only mum and dad watching by now, aye? That eruption has got the world distracted." He cut the feed on his phone and removed the GoPro from his head, stuffing it into the hoodie pocket as he put the torn halves back on. They clambered back to their feet and moved to where they could see what was happening at the volcano's crater. They watched it for just seconds until Brodie got them moving, rapidly retracing the path back to the Land Rover. He explained they had little time before ash and lahars could come down from the eruption.

Ruth called them and was put on speaker. In a rush of communication, she praised them for finding and saving Maya. She explained she had Brodie's truck and was getting in it now and following the evacuation drill, driving out of town like everyone else. As she spoke, she looked out of the window of the truck up at the mountain.

"Guys, um, that ash cloud is starting to fall down the mountain now… Are you at the Land Rover?"

"No," Ken replied, looking at the clear sky through the foliage. They moved around to again see the mountain top through the leaves. That was when they witnessed a wall of ash and falling debris rushing down the mountain toward them.

"If you're where I think you are," she cried, "you've got to run! You've got no time!"

CHAPTER THIRTY-ONE

They took off, crashing through the brush as fast as their exhausted bodies could go.

Maya discovered her adrenaline was spent, and the renewed panic gave her no new energy. Her starved body felt heavy and would not respond to her internal screams to make it flee. She tried to run but fell twice, getting up and moving again, unable to keep their pace. She looked back up at the mountain, and where earlier it was a serrated snow-capped top that had turned into a powerful eruption, now all she saw was a tsunami of ash rushing toward her. She felt the terror return, but her body could not respond.

Brodie came back to her. "Get on my back!" he demanded, kneeling down,

Maya found the energy to leap on, gripping his thick neck with her small arms. He stood up and showing little sign of the weight he was carrying, continued forward, crashing through shrubs and thickets like the rugby player he was, cutting around corners and between trees, like he was slicing through a defensive line. Sabre raced ahead with barks and yelps.

Glancing back, Ken saw the thick cloud of ash just a couple of hundred meters behind them, billowing down the mountainside, making everything disappear in its path. Maya held on as tight as she could, seeing the foliage whip by as Brodie went down declines with huge bounds and scrambled up inclines with his hands pulling at the roots and branches for leverage. He was sweating and panting heavily, but did not slow.

They came around an outcropping and saw the familiar scene where Brodie had released the kiwis and where the vehicles lay a hundred meters ahead. Behind them was the roar of the ash and rocks coming down, with branches snapping like twigs and foliage being buried. The sound overwhelmed all senses, like being at the bottom of a cataract falling into a ravine.

As they reached the vehicles, the cloud hit them like a wave on a beach. Ash and rocks rained through the canopy, branches, and leaves snapping. Their vision almost disappeared. "Get their water and food!" Brodie ordered, pulling open the back of the Russian's van. Maya fell off his back into the van, grabbing at whatever packages of food and several bottles of water she could see. She passed these to Brodie, and he ran to the Land Rover, which Ken was opening, letting Sabre jump in.

They all climbed in and slammed the doors. The inside was now a thick cloud of ash, and they were coughing and choking, trying to catch their breath in the acrid air. Something heavy slammed onto the roof of the vehicle, causing a large dent above their heads, and the vehicle swayed on its suspension. Other smaller rocks began to crash into the roof and windscreen, like bullets hitting metal and glass. Cracks began to form on the windows as pellets of rock rained down on them.

"Get us under some cover!" Brodie yelled, pulling a piece of his hoodie over his mouth.

Ken started the vehicle, and it sputtered to life, straining from the ash in the air that overwhelmed the engine filters. He put it in gear and started the windshield wipers to try to remove some of the ash and debris continuing to pour over the vehicle. He put it in drive and hit the gas. The vehicle shot forward, a moment later hitting the berm. They lurched back in their seats as it climbed up over the edge. He drove several meters into the thicket of trees and shrubs, the vehicle straining to push against the foliage, and then came to a stop. He killed the engine, and they were suddenly engulfed in a whiteout. Pellets continued to fall down on them like a hailstorm, and they heard larger branches snapping and falling under the weight of the downpour. Each of them was coughing and wheezing, trying to cover their mouths with their garments and see through squinted eyes.

Ken called Ruth on speaker who picked up immediately. "*Are you in the vehicle?!*" she asked. They could hear the grind of the gears as she was driving.

"Yeah! It's a crap storm here!" (*cough*) Ken yelled back. "We're choking," (*cough*).

"*Pull out the red emergency kit in the back! There are gas masks, goggles, an oxygen tank, and a hand-cranking gadget to charge a phone and has a radio, light, blah, blah, blah."* As she was speaking Maya clambered into the back of the Land Rover, finding the kit. *"Put a wet shirt around Sabre's mouth and force him to breath only through it. Keep wetting it, but don't drown him."*

Maya pulled the kit open and began distributing pieces as fast as she could.

In minutes they were all breathing properly through masks with goggles on. Brodie tied a wet cloth around Sabre's jaw, which, after wrestling with the dog to keep it on him, finally gained his cooperation.

Slowly the hailstorm of rocks began to abate as the ash piled up thicker and thicker. They heard large branches and trees crash around them. A few trees landed heavily on the Land Rover, bouncing them on the vehicle's suspension.

The faint light from the windows gradually disappeared, and then they were in darkness.

Ken turned on the emergency light and adjusted the oxygen tank to give them a faint flow they could breathe from. In the kit they found a first-aid bag and applied ointments and bandages to Maya's wrists and some of the bleeding cuts on their exposed skin.

They used some of the water to rinse their mouths, drink, and wipe their face and hands.

Maya found her camera and bag sitting on the seat and switched out her camera's battery. She took photos of them in the muted yellow light with gas masks and goggles on, buried in ash.

"How did you find me?" she asked through the mask.

Ken pulled her camera strap out of his back pocket and held it up. "Sabre found you."

Her eyes teared up again, and she gave the dog a long hug.

She then snuggled up to Ken. Within seconds she had fallen asleep in his arms.

CHAPTER THIRTY-TWO

Ruth and Cynthia stood together, watching in the early morning light as the large red rescue helicopter lifted itself off from the ground of the disaster coordination site and pulled into the sky. It turned and headed to the mountain location of the Land Rover. They gazed around in awe at the scene of hundreds of vehicles and people erecting makeshift hospitals, tents, and food distribution centers. What was once a large open field in front of the Chateau Tongariro, several kilometers north of the volcano had become a coordinated rescue and recovery center.

She and Cynthia had spent a few hours of the night on cots in a Chateau conference hall that had been reconfigured in a matter of hours. The huge building was upwind from the flow of ash that continued to fall. Built over a hundred years ago, it stood alone in the middle of the countryside as a grand chateau with over a hundred hotel rooms.

After an hour of continued eruptions, the volcano had quieted down to a steady stream of white smoke that continued to still pour into the sky, like smoking embers after a bonfire. The snow on the mountain was gone, evaporated, or covered under a thick layer of ash. As the snow and ice melted under the heat of the debris, lahars formed in several places that came tearing down the mountain. These had followed predicted paths, moving thousands of tons of mud, rock, and water every second, that dug new channels in riverbeds and washed away the banks, spilling over into fields and washing away many square kilometers of trees and shrubs. Several homes were lost, and overspill had swamped several roads. Rescue crews were already working to clear them with backhoes and dirt movers as the flow of the lahars abated. Aerial shots of the damage posted on the GeoNet website showed Ruth the town of Ohakune, and her own home lodge were spared. The worst she could expect was her garden and home exterior ruined under a thin layer of ash.

During the evening, several rescue helicopters had arrived along with hundreds of emergency vehicles, rescue workers and government officials to coordinate the necessary rescue and clean-up efforts. The playbook for such a natural disaster, already worked out in detail and updated regularly, had gone into action.

Ruth had stayed in comm with the three trapped in her Land Rover, ensuring they were able to breathe and hydrate. They sent selfies, which Ruth shared with the growing list of followers at the Chateau Rentals Facebook site, which was now well over eight figures and continuing to climb.

It was now dawn, and recovery efforts were in full swing. The two ladies reentered the tent that had been set up to coordinate the rescue efforts, a makeshift panel of flat screens and computer monitors displaying real-time events as workers searched for survivors under ash and attempted to reopen roads and establish essential supply lines. Working with the site coordinator, they updated the Land Rover occupants on what was happening and what to expect.

The place where the Land Rover was buried was unrecognizable from the day before. All the foliage and vegetation that had covered that area of the mountain was gone, flattened under a thick layer of ash half a meter deep. The vehicle was just a bulge on the ground a little ways from a larger bulge that was the van. Tree trunks, stripped bare of branches and leaves, dotted the landscape like the aftermath of a nuclear explosion.

A Channel 3 news helicopter hovered further back, its powerful cameras zoomed in on the scene, feeding humankind's unquenchable appetite for sensational news.

The rescue helicopter hovered above as two rescue workers in full-body orange hazmat suits with built-in gas masks descended from cables to the ground with a case of equipment on a separate line. The powerful blades beat the air down upon the site, causing a cloud of ash to billow out from the edges. Arriving on the ground, the rescue workers unclipped themselves and their equipment, and the lines were reeled back in as the helicopter pulled back. The two workers waded through the knee high ash to the vehicle, pulling their supplies behind them.

Ruth watched on the newsfeed as they pulled out spades and began to dig around the vehicle. They used electric saws to cut away and remove branches, making their way through the thick layers of ash, like digging a car out from a blizzard. She kept Ken on speaker as he reported they were starting to see the light through the windows and cheered when the first worker was able to see them in the window and wave to them.

Fifteen minutes later they were being individually strapped into harnesses and pulled up into the helicopter. Brodie held onto Sabre who was tied to his body. Maya continued to take photos of the rescue operation and surrounding landscape with her camera as she was pulled up into the belly of the chopper.

As each person was freed from the site, cheers went up from the people around Ruth and Cynthia. They hugged each other and wiped away tears of joy. They could hear similar cheering from different sections of the disaster coordination sight as people followed the successful rescue on their hand-held devices.

A deep sense of relief swept through Ruth.

CHAPTER THIRTY-THREE

Two days later Ruth, Cynthia, and the three survivors emerged from the entrance of the Wellington Regional Hospital, greeted by a crowd of well-wishers, media, and government officials. Bandages covered arms and legs, but they were smiling and walking fine.

Media around the world had been covering their story, along with the volcanic eruption, now recorded as the largest in a century for New Zealand. It was reported that with the emergency drill in place and preparedness of the region, only three lives were yet confirmed as lost in the eruption. These were the three Russians, whose bodies had been washed downstream in a lahar, found ten kilometers from where they had fallen into a collapsed gorge.

The rescue helicopter had taken Ken, Maya, and Brodie to the Chateau Tongariro emergency grounds, where, after a short stop and triage inspection, they had been transferred to another helicopter along with Ruth and Cynthia and taken down to Wellington for treatment of multiple abrasions and smoke inhalation.

Ruth's immediate family had come down to Wellington by private plane, arranged for by the government. They were there, her daughter, son-in-law, and three young grandchildren, standing by waiting SUVs and clapping with the rest of the crowd. Her oldest grandchild, Tessy, had Sabre on a leash, the dog having been professionally groomed and sporting a new collar. Tessy had tried to do her best to hold Sabre still for photographers, but the dog was not so willing to listen to her commands and appeared eager to be reunited with its owner. She answered simple questions about him from the media and adoring public, including many times making up answers to make the dog look even smarter and herself more knowledgable, which got a laugh from her mother.

Also there was Ken's sister, Jane Ryan, who had booked an Air New Zealand flight from Los Angeles to Auckland shortly after being included in the email blast from Ruth and had seen her brother become buried in ash. The evening flight from LAX had brought her into Auckland early that very morning, just in time to catch the same private flight along with the rest of her New Zealand family.

A microphone stand had been set up in anticipation of speeches being made, but other than one by the Prime Minister an hour earlier, none of them showed an interest.

They stood at the entrance, accepting handshakes of congratulations, and meekly waved to the crowd as they slowly moved down the sidewalk to the SUVs. Ken and Maya held hands, embarrassed by all the attention.

Brodie, his arm around Kayana, recognized his father and uncle, standing solemnly in full Maori regalia. A group of other tribal men stood at attention behind them. His parents had visited him the night before in the hospital, along with a cavalcade of relatives bringing praise, food, and gifts. Now his father looked regal and serious, masking a glowing feeling of intense pride.

Stepping forward, his father's voice boomed over the crowd.

The clapping and cheering hushed. Several cameras and all attention turned to him.

He took another step toward his son, raising a taiaha above his head. He skillfully twirled it and then while advancing with balanced motions on the balls of his feet, whipped it forward in a threatening stance. A dozen other members of the tribe came behind him in unison, following his lead.

Kayana put a hand to her chest and tried to control her breathing to steady her emotions. Brodie slowly shook his head, overpowered by the symbology and spiritual meaning of the gesture. He choked up, his lip trembling as tears fell down his cheeks.

The Haka began...

Kapa o pango kia whakawhenua au i ahau!
Hi aue, hi!
Ko Aotearoa e ngunguru nei!...

(Let me go back to my first gasp of breath

It is New Zealand that thunders now...)

ABOUT THE AUTHOR

Jesse Reiss was born in England to an American father and New Zealand mother. As a citizen of both countries, he has traveled widely in each. He lives in Los Angeles with his wife.